THE UNDEAD THAT SAV
VAMPIRE EDITION

EDITED BY
LYLE PEREZ-TINICS &
JOE FILIPPONE

Rainstorm Press
PO BOX 391038
Anza, Ca 92539
www.RainstormPress.com

ISBN 10 – 1-937758-03-6
ISBN 13 – 978-1-937758-03-5

Library of Congress: 2011960999

THE UNDEAD THAT SAVED CHRISTMAS: VAMPIRE EDITION

Rainstorm Press http://www.RainstormPress.com
Copyright © 2011 by Rainstorm Press
All rights reserved

Interior design by –
THE MAD FORMATTER
www.TheMadFormatter.com

Cover illustration by Robert Elrod
www.RobertElrodLLC.com

This book is dedicated to the foster kids at
Hugs Foster Family Agency
http://www.HugsFFA.org

Acknowledgment
Net proceeds from this book will be donated to Hugs Foster Family Agency. No author or illustrator has been compensated for their time and efforts. Our payment is to help provide their foster children with a wonderful Christmas

Table of Contents
Stories and Poems

Comics

Introduction
By David Wellington, author of Thirteen Bullets

Ah, Christmas! Is there any better time to be a blood-sucking vampire?

Think about it—it's one of the longest nights of the year. The streets are deserted and all the helpless little mortals are hiding in their homes. The kids are upstairs in bed, with orders not to come out of their rooms no matter what they hear. Mom's in the back room desperately trying to get all the presents wrapped. She's far too busy to suspect a thing. And Dad... well, Dad's already had three spiked egg nogs and is sprawled out, half conscious, in front of the TV*. Put on a red suit and a beard and he'll invite you in with open arms!

My guess is that there are two kinds of people reading these words right now. Group One are the normal, decent kind of folk who are looking for a present to get someone else. They have the grave misfortune of having a dark, brooding weirdo for a brother or a cousin or a podiatrist, someone who likes creepy stories about nasty vampires (we'll call *those* people Group Two). Yuck, right? Not your kind of thing at all. That first paragraph up there made you want to go take a shower (especially if you read the footnote). But read this next section—I promise, it'll make you feel a lot better:

Christmas. It's a wonderful time for vampires... and for families. For some of us it's the one time of year we get to go home and be with our loved ones. The time when we can re-connect, catch up on what's happened in our busy years. A time when we share far more than presents and songs and corny old traditions.

It's a time when we celebrate the bonds that hold us together. When we honor the sacrifices of those who raised us, who gave up so much so we could have a better life. The parents

---

* It's a well known fact that vampires don't drink... wine. What is far less well known is that vampires can, indeed, get drunk, as long as they prey on victims with a significant blood alcohol content.

who were there for us when we cried and when we had our first triumphs, who fed and clothed us for so many years when we couldn't look after ourselves.

Of course, not everyone is lucky enough to have that. There are far too many kids who don't have a mom or a dad to be with in the holiday season.

That's where this book comes in.

The Undead Who Saved Christmas: Vampire Edition is a charity anthology of stories, poems and comics that helps support Hugs Foster Family Agency, an organization devoted to finding safe, nurturing homes for every child regardless of their circumstances. Hugs FFA is there to help the kids who would otherwise slip through the cracks—kids who need intensive care or supervision, kids who have nowhere else to go. They are a vital resource and by buying this book you're helping make their work possible.

There, wasn't that nice? If you're in Group One, now you know why you should buy this book. Your obligation is complete; wrap the book up so you don't have to look at that cover anymore, send it to the dark, brooding weirdo who runs your nail salon or grooms your pets, and don't think about it again. Please, please don't read any further.

As for Group Two... well, let's take a second and make sure Group One has stopped reading. Hey, now, nice normal people—no fair peeking! The rest of this book is for Group Two only. Good. They're gone, right?

The Undead Who Saved Christmas: Vampire Edition is a great stocking stuffer, and a perfect gift for dark, brooding weirdoes everywhere. Now that we're the only ones in the room...

The works you're about to experience are grim. They are nasty and violent and dark. These aren't the kind of Christmas vampire stories you may be used to, where the vampire sees the cherubic faces of the caroling children and the love and warmth of the season and repents his evil ways. This book doesn't contain a single story about a vampire who goes around giving treats to good little boys and girls while riding in a magical sleigh. Well... actually, there are a couple stories

8

here like that... but they don't exactly have happy endings.

Nor are there any stories in here about sparkling vampires who fall deeply in love with girls one tenth their age for reasons nobody can guess. Okay, actually, there's one poem like that. But it's one of the more twisted pieces in the anthology, I promise.

What this anthology does contain is comics. Comics! It's rare to see comics included in a work like this, and very welcome. The editors have collected three of the most twisted works of Christmas-themed sequential art I've ever seen.

In fact the editors have gone to some length to bring you only the most grotesque, maniacal, *depraved* stories they could find. Every piece here is designed to make you cringe, to make you shudder, to make you lock the doors and wear a necklace of garlic cloves everywhere you go (note: this probably won't help against vampires, but it will help you meet other like-minded dark, brooding weirdoes).

I won't keep you any longer. If I know my dark, brooding weirdoes (and I should, since I am one myself) you're probably not even reading this right now. You were probably in too great a hurry to jump in and get to the nasty parts. Well, have at it. Turn the page and find out why Christmas is every vampire's new favorite holiday. Go indulge your sick little fetish for blood and guts, you lunatic.

But know, as you do so, that you've done a good deed and maybe even helped make some kid's Christmas a little brighter. I know, I know, the very thought makes your skin crawl. But on behalf of the kids, and everyone involved in this project. Thank you. And have a very happy holiday.

LET THE MAYHEM BEING

Story Art Cover

By Cinsearae S.
http://BloodTouch.webs.com

Dedication

For those who have lost the Christmas spirit for whatever reason you may have, may this story offer a spark of hope for humanity.

Author Bio

Ms. Cinsearae S. is the Editor/Publisher of award-winning **Dark Gothic Resurrected Magazine** and a graphic designer for **Damnation Books** and independent authors. Author of **The Abraxas Series** and **Boleyn: Tudor Vampire**, she is also the proprietor of **Mistress Rae's Decadent Designs** on Etsy.com. Cinsearae is an avid lover of all things gothic and horrific, and is a huge Vincent Price fan. She lives with her husband and two rat terriers, aptly names Hades and Chaos. Visit her at http://BloodTouch.webs.com or find her on Facebook and Twitter.

A Miracle Of Mercy
By Cinsearae S.

He was awakened by a chill that was colder than usual. It swept over his entire body, causing an uncomfortable stiffness that pained him to the marrow. The first muscles to move were those in his face as his mouth curled into a snarl of disgust. The extreme coldness told him one thing. It was *that* time of year again.

He took a deep, labored breath, icy air filling his dead lungs, as the noise that escaped his lips sounded more like a wheeze. Soil poured into his mouth, and he coughed. His fingers twitched, grasping at the damp dirt around him. His coffin had been through years of earthly wear and tear; the wood encasing his body warped and rotted with time, full of holes from the merciless gnawing of insects.

He despised waking up during the winter season. It only made it harder for him to return back to his dreamless slumber. He still wondered why he had been damned to such a life, but a nagging thought in the back of his mind always reminded him that it was because of the listless, pitiless life he lived.

It came as no surprise to him when people avoided him while he was alive. He was misanthropic, viewing people as nothing but mindless, simpering, self-absorbed dolts, eager to please only themselves. They were greedy, inconsiderate of others, rude, and faceless. He saw no point in associating with people of such stature. Humankind bored him as well as annoyed him. The only things he ever loved were his wife and daughter.

The energies of the Christmas season were such a nuisance. Humans had turned a holiday of mirth, thanks, and love into one of commercialism and avarice. There was more negativity in the air during this time of year than any other, and it resonated deep into the ground where he slept; a dull murmur that entered his ears, waking his brain from his yearly slumber.

Knowing that he would be unable to go back to sleep, he began to claw his way to the earth's surface, cursing the world

15

as he did so. He emerged from a churchyard, shaking newly-fallen snow from his matted hair.

His body felt stiffer with every passing year, and every year he damned being bound to the earth for his cold, uncaring ways. His last memories while alive were of it being Christmas Eve. It was snowing hard, and he had just left a tavern. A young and stupid teen was speeding down the street and struck him; his body crumpling and flying over the car's windshield. He awoke in his coffin exactly one year later, on the date of his death, bewildered and confused, not to mention terrifying everyone he came across. With no mirror to see himself, he didn't realize he bore the pallor of the living dead. With eyes and skin that matched the icy, grayish-white season, his tattered funeral garments provided little resistance to the cold, not that he needed it.

He also did not understand his sudden urge to snatch a stray dog into an alley and tear into its throat, gorging himself with its life's essence. The thick ruby-red substance filled his stomach as he drank, and he felt relief from the gnawing pain in his stomach. A passer-by spotted him in the alley and screamed, running away as he hissed at her, bearing blood-stained fangs.

This ritual continued year after year: rising on Christmas Eve, grabbing his first meal of the night, wreaking havoc every time anyone dared to bother him, and finally returning to his grave before the holiday came to close the following night.

This time, however, his clothing was in mere tatters. He'd be nearly naked if not for a few strategically placed pieces. Even the soles of his shoes had his feet touching the ground. He staggered his way to a thrift store, where a few donation bins outside of the building were overflowing with forgotten garments. As he walked, he commanded his joints to become limber; he felt more like a revenant than a vampire.

A few derelicts were at the bins, picking through clothing that would possibly fit them. They didn't even bother to look up at the oncoming stranger. As he walked, he couldn't help but chuckle to himself. People had become so egocentric over the years, they couldn't even sense when they were in danger, whether they were young or old, rich or poor. Nearly drooling, he could almost taste their blood flowing from their veins into his awaiting mouth.

Once upon the crowd, about to attack, one of them tossed him a brown wool coat. He caught it effortlessly, almost taken aback.

"Looks like you need that more than us," one of them said. The derelict didn't face him directly; he merely glanced him over. Still, the vampire was astounded that someone actually showed concern for someone other than themselves.

He nodded at the derelict and threw the coat on. It hung loosely on his thin frame, due to his continuing desiccation, but it was better that it was too large than too small. He decided to spare the homeless group from their deadly demise and traveled onward.

Stores had their Christmas lights adorning the windows and doors with their rainbow array of colors. Street poles were wrapped with pine garland, thick red-and-gold ribbons, and huge bows to match. From out of a few bars, he could hear the all too-tired Christmas classics of *Santa Baby*, *Rudolph The Red Nosed Reindeer*, *O, Holy Night*, and *Little Drummer Boy* all meshed together in a single, annoying din. He gritted his teeth so hard, one of his molars cracked. He didn't even flinch from the pain, but someone would have thought he was in pain anyway, with how he grimaced at the cheerful melodies. He absolutely *hated* Christmas, despising the fact that he woke up every year like clockwork and dealt with the hassle of it all.

He walked along the slushy sidewalk, a few adults running like chickens with their heads cut off, trying to buy last-minute gifts. A few rushed by, bumping into him, not even bothering to apologize. He growled, the noise catching the attention of one of them. A young man in his twenties.

"Fuck off old man, or get out of the way!" He smirked and continued walking down the street.

'I'll show you an old man,' he thought, skulking off into an alley, moving with fluid speed. He caught the young man at the opposite end, stepping out from the darkness and right into his path. The young man stumbled back, surprised.

"What the--?" His jaw dropped, incredulous to whom he was seeing in front of him. "I left you back there!" He pointed up the street as he trembled in nervousness. "How'd you---?"

The vampire grabbed him by the collar and shoved him

back into the alley, slamming him against the brick wall, raising him off his feet a few inches.

"Where's your **soul** boy?" He snarled, his eyes glowing a solid red. The young man was speechless. "You, who cares for nothing; too cold to be considerate, too blind to the world's decay. You *all* are nothing but worthless *parasites!*"

The young man scrunched his face up in terror. "Please, let me go...let me go!"

The vampire looked down at the small bag in the man's hand. With his other free hand, he snatched the bag from him. He took out a very small, colorful wrapped box, in pink paper with a royal blue ribbon, and shook it to his ear. Something tumbled about inside.

"Who is this for?" He asked in a gravelly voice, still staring at the present.

"M-my girlfriend. Please Sir, I'm sorry, just let me go. I'll give you money if that's what you want!"

"Let you go? Why, when we're getting along *so* well?" He chuckled, then gave a big smile, exposing rows of pointed teeth to his victim.

The young man screamed as the vampire lurched forward, tearing into his neck. Blood spurted from his wound like a fountain, splashing onto both of them. Once he had his fill, he dropped the man to the ground like an unwanted rag doll, and wiped the blood from his mouth with the back of his hand. He looked at the spattered red mess on his collar and frowned.

"And I was beginning to *like* this coat," he mumbled to himself.

He looked down at the dead body at his feet, bent over, and removed a wallet from the man's back pocket. He flipped it open, reading his driver's license, making a mental note of his home address, then picked up the gift he intended to give his girlfriend, and pocketed it. He'd be paying her a visit soon enough. Why *not* spread the love he had just bestowed to her boyfriend, to *her* as well? 'Tis the season to be giving, wasn't it?

* * *

The moon was round and full in the sky, but the vampire couldn't even see its glow for all the garish Christmas lights

18

coming from every direction. A homey, little bistro had the most wonderful smells of butter cookies, chocolate, and hazelnut coffee wafting from its location, inviting many people in to warm up and sit for a while. He glanced into the windows from a distance, watching people talk amongst each other, tons of shopping bags at their feet, munching on goodies or sipping drinks from their mugs. He could hear the buzz of many conversations, most of them bitching and complaining about gifts they had to buy for their ungrateful children or picky significant others, problems with returning items after the holidays, getting hideous, unwanted, or useless gifts, the impersonal feel of getting a mere gift card, or the insult of getting a present that was re-gifted back to the same person who gave it.

He leaned against a pole that was wrapped in gold-colored garland and a few glass ornaments, listening to their idle chatter. The garland made a crunchy sound as he crushed it, and he rolled his eyes. He snatched it off the pole, popping it in half, and draped it around his neck as a sort of mockery. The ornaments had dropped to the ground, two of them breaking with a tiny *clink* against the icy patches of sidewalk. Sounds of, *Oh Come, Ye Merry Gentlemen* drifted from a small speaker hanging outside of the shop. The vampire grimaced again.

"Merry? *Merry*? There is nothing *merry* about this time of year," he said to himself, then glanced at the smashed ornaments on the ground. One of them managed not to break. It was an angel, blowing into a trumpet. He picked it up, observing it closely, deciding to hold onto it as he made his way into the shop.

The little bell that hung over the door tinkled as the vampire walked in. Without a word, he flipped over the sign hanging on the door that read "OPEN", to make it read "CLOSED". Immediately, all chatter fell silent as everyone stared at this hideous-looking, homeless person that smelled as fetid as a sewage plant. The owners of the shop wanted to tell him to leave, but their words were caught in their throats. There was something about this man that made everyone's blood run cold.

The vampire smiled at their obliviousness, and purposely took a seat at an empty table right in the middle of the shop. He observed the looks on everyone's faces, from dumbfounded to disgusted. He narrowed his eyes at them all, giving a mocking grin, then ignored them for a moment as he fished through his coat pocket for the angel ornament. Once it was in his grip, he gently placed it on the table before him, and stared at it for a moment. The silence in the shop was so deafening, the dripping sounds of the coffeemakers could be heard.

His deathly stench slowly began to overpower the sweet, hearth-like scents of the shop, but the people dared not to make a move. Still staring at the angel, the vampire spoke to no one in particular. "Care to offer a penniless man a cup of tea?"

One of the workers behind the counter went to work right away preparing a mug for him. The vampire grinned as the counter guy briskly walked over to his table and placed the tea before him.

"A-anything else, sir?" He asked, wringing his hands in nervousness.

The vampire glanced up at his host with steely, grey eyes and gave a quick sniff in his direction. "No my boy, but please, be calm... you reek of fear."

A patron towards the back of the shop snorted at the remark and leaned towards her friend. "The only thing that reeks is *him*," she whispered. Naturally, the vampire heard it.

"And it is your very demeanor that reeks most of *all*," he retorted, staring directly at her. The woman swallowed hard and kept her mouth shut. He continued looking at the rest of the crowd, into the empty eyes of so many empty people.

"You humans are more lifeless than I am. How ironic it is to see that the dead are more alive than the living." He fiddled with the angel on the table for a moment. "What does this symbolize?" The vampire asked, picking it up and showing it to everyone. "What does this represent to you?"

Everyone remained silent, so he rolled his eyes.

"Please people, this is not a trick question... or are you all too *stupid* to answer?"

"They're messengers of God," a young boy replied, and the vampire smiled.

"Very good, my young man. I wonder why no *adult* could answer that one simple question." He leered at the patrons of the shop again before placing the angel back on the table, gazing at it once more.

"Messengers of God..." he said to himself, his voice trailing off. "Spreaders of good tidings and joy. Messengers of love, hope and faith. Isn't Christmastide a time for such things... as it *should* be *year 'round*?"

In one swift motion, he brought his hand down on the ornament, smashing it into pieces. Parts of the angel skittered across the table and fell to the floor. The people jumped in surprise and small murmurs of nervousness could be heard.

"You all make me *sick*," he spat, his incisors slowly extending in repulsion. "Through the years, you humans besmirched the true meaning of this time of year with your materialism, your gluttony, your senseless minds for '*me, me, me*' and, '*I want, I want I want*'! I can't *stand* to hear your weak and petty whining for more, more, more, when there are so many others out there who wish they could have an *iota* of the things you use in one month, and dispose of in the next! You've lost the meaning of charity, kindness and goodwill, either hoarding things you'll never use, or throwing them away, when they could be given to those in need! To give something out of the pure kindness of your heart doesn't *exist*. Anything that *is* given comes with a price, doesn't it? Gifts have become bribes, tokens from debtors, and trinkets from apologetic persons to alleviate the guilt of something they've done wrong! What happened to the spirit of giving simply for the *joy* of it?"

Not a single person could answer him.

"Your conversations are laughable, making me shake my head in utter *pity*." He looked over to one woman who had a very chiseled, stern face. "I've never seen or heard people stress themselves silly over such trivial things--wanting to impress a houseful of strangers with their Christmas parties, worrying whether the tablecloth and napkin rings will match or not, hoping a guest will not be wearing the same dress as they will, or begrudging an invitation to a couple they don't deem worthy enough of attending. Such *conceitedness* and *arrogance*," he hissed, continuing to glance over the anxious people, settling on a gentleman in his twenties.

"Or *you*---your guilt simply roils over you... buying your girlfriend several presents to assuage her suspicions of the deception you've cleverly played against her...by having an affair with another behind her back." The vampire mockingly shook his finger at him. "For shame, young man... but I've seen that this is a game that many humans play with each other these days. Commitment and dedication is a joke in everyone's eyes."

He looked at the palm of his hand, his dead blood congealing on his cold, hard skin. He smeared it across the table top. The people grimaced at his actions.

"And sadly, these are same deceptive, superficial behaviors you bestow on your progeny, only to have *them* grow up and become exact copies of yourselves. Worthless... insubstantial... without merit." His dead-cold glare was even more deadly as his irises became a dark shade of red--a horrible, stark contrast to his white skin. The people began to scream and run around haphazardly as he jumped up without warning and attacked everyone in the shop.

Outside, if anyone had been around, they would have seen large streaks of red continuously splattering against the large windows of the coffee shop, the terrified faces of the patrons, bags and presents flying everywhere as people trampled over one another to get away, and one lone vampire quickly pulling down the Venetian blinds in order to finish off his ghastly feast of blood in total privacy.

When the melee was over, the vampire exited the shop as if nothing had ever happened, quietly closing the door behind him. He kicked a bloodied teddy bear down the steps. The lower half of his face and neck was a ruddy mess, the lapels of his coat so soaked with his victims' blood that they looked black.

"Such stupid, insignificant sheep," he mumbled, walking down the icy sidewalk, gleefully kicking the teddy bear a few more times before landing it on a sewer grate.

He did, however, spare the one boy who answered his question with honesty. As he stared hard into the child's eyes, he could tell the boy hadn't been marred by the twisted and paltry mentality of society, and could only hope he'd remain that way. There was also something about the boy's eyes that sent the slightest of shivers down the vampire's spine, but he shook it off as he turned his back on him. He still wasn't quite finished with spreading his own version of Christmas cheer.

* * *

The vampire made his way down the street, coming across a church. He could hear a Christmas Eve candlelight service going on inside, harmonious music emanating all around the grounds. He found a back entranceway into the building, sneaking inside. He watched as the priest stood at the front of the congregation, everyone holding a lit candle in their hands as he spoke.

"Blessed be our Heavenly Father. Born to us was His son who would bring the light, love and joy of His teachings to the world. And blessed be the Heavenly hosts, who would--"

The priest choked and gurgled on his next word, blood draining from his lips and down his robe as the congregation shrieked. All they could see were two grimy, veined, grayish-white arms reaching around the priest, grabbing him, and then a quick flash of a head leaning forward and biting into his neck.

When the vampire got his fill, he dropped the priest with a thud, the crowd still yelling and shrieking, wondering what evil, foul *thing* had entered their peaceful sanctuary on such a holy night.

The vampire looked out at the panic-stricken crowd that was reacting as badly as frightened cattle. He then glanced over at a nativity scene off to the side of the pulpit, and slowly stagger to it.

He stared at the baby in the manger, his mind suddenly awash in far-away thoughts of a time when things were much simpler, much more enjoyable.

And then he recalled the day when his daughter Josephine was born.

He remembered when he held her tiny body in his hands for the very first time as his wife passed on, making him promise to take good care of her. He recalled himself crying as he kissed his daughter's forehead in sadness and joy, as he held her close. He lost one love, but gained another, and would fulfill his vow to his wife.

He watched Josephine grow, shared every birthday with her, proud of every good grade she got in her classes, watched as she received honors in high school, and as valedictorian, gave the class graduation speech. And then, his pride and joy

Cinsearae S.

had been snatched away from him by an arrogant young man while she was in college. She left everything to be with this pompous fool. A career. A good job. A great future.

Even him.

His life was never the same after that. He kept himself estranged from the world and his only child. Was *this* his reward for her care? Loneliness? Total abandon? Loss?

He threw himself back into the work-force to keep his mind off of things. He befriended no one. His daughter called, wrote, and sent cards every year, but he ignored them all, too busy and too bitter to respond. Then one day, all the calls, letters and cards had stopped. She had finally given up. He realized it one snowy, Christmas Eve, when he noticed the absence of a light pink envelope he always got in the mail. He went to his room and opened a drawer, where he kept Josephine's cards and letters tucked away, all of them unopened. Giving a small noise of despair, he gathered them up, sorting them by year, month and date. Then, he opened every one of them, starting from the beginning.

The earlier letters were full of joy. Brian, her boyfriend, as well as herself, were graduating top honors from college. They were each guaranteed a good job upon getting their degrees. The letters progressed as to how well they were doing, although she was disappointed at her father for not showing up at graduation. Within a year, they had bought a house, and were thinking about starting a family. She also wished he would write back to her or call, wondering why he hadn't, and hoped he was doing okay.

The letters continued. Their jobs were great, they had a golden retriever now--Josephine's favorite dog--and she talked about various trips they had taken across the states and even a few getaway vacations. The way she described how beautiful each place was, he felt as if he was right there with her. And for the first time, he cracked just the slightest smile.

And then, the biggest surprise of all. Josephine had found out she was pregnant. His smile faltered. Her job and career were put on hold indefinitely. But Brian continued to be ever-faithful, ever-loving, showering her with the best gifts money could buy, and they continued living in happiness.

She often described how the baby would feel moving around

24

in her, as if excited to see the world. She'd talk about her plans and dreams for the child, wondered what type of life it would live. If it was a girl, she'd name it after her mom whom she never met--Amelia. And if it were a boy, she'd name it after him, her dad--James.

Tears fell from his eyes after reading this, but he continued on.

Eventually, the baby came. It *was* a boy, so James he was named. Josephine couldn't help but express her disappointment in her father's continued absence in her life, as well as his grandson's, and he began feeling the pangs of regret and despair. He even noticed a few tear stains on the letters she had written to him. Although everything was described in great detail, and with photos included, he had missed James' birth, first birthday, first steps, first day to pre-school, second birthday, first time on a tricycle...

He crushed the letter to his chest. He had been such a total fool. Although he despised the man his daughter was with, he left himself out of her life out of sheer anger. Who was he to tell her how to live her own life? She was free to make her own choices. He may not have liked them all, but it was no reason to estrange himself from her. His only child. And now, she had a family of her own, and he had estranged himself from that as well!

As he kept reading, he also noticed her growing distress in Brian not showing an interest in marrying her yet. It was as if everything had fallen into place *but* that. And every time, Brian had some sort of excuse. The job was about to call him away to work in another state for a while, or money was a little tight right then for a big wedding... but Josephine didn't care about a 'big' wedding; just a simple "I do" at a Justice of the Peace would have been suffice. So Brian made promise after promise that they'd discuss their wedding plans in detail, but never did.

His anger started to grow again as he kept reading.

Brian's job kept calling him away more and more frequently, leaving her alone with the baby. Josephine's mounting anxiety compelled her to hire a private investigator. When Brian was called for a job that required being out-of-state again, the private investigator was on the case. After a month, the investigator returned to Josephine, revealing several photos of Brian with another woman at fancy restaurants late at night, going into the woman's home and leaving early in the morning, and sometimes her joining *him* in his hotel room for days at a time. The investigator also managed to get recordings of a few phone calls between the two of them. Either Brian had lied about having a woman in his life already and being a father as well, or the woman knew and simply didn't care. Either way, they spoke back and forth to each other as if *they* were man and wife.

And not *once* did he leave for an out-of-state job that month.

Josephine was devastated, numbed to all feeling. No wonder he had no desire to get married. It would only entail him having to give up alimony--which meant half of everything he owned--and he was not about to do that.

In his eyes, he was playing it smart.

Josephine left a trail of the investigator's photos all over the house, leaving no place where Brian would miss seeing one. She left a note on the kitchen table saying she didn't want to see his face when she got back, took their son, and stayed at a motel for a few days. It was during this point in time that she wrote to her father more frequently asking for advice. After six letters in one week's time, she wrote that she couldn't understand what she did to her father to deserve such coldness from him in return. Little James was five now, still not sure what was going on with mommy and daddy, but knew enough to know something was very, very wrong.

That happened in the spring, just before the Easter holiday. There were no more letters, calls, or cards after that.

This was also the same year he didn't receive a pink envelope. Each one always contained a handmade Christmas card. They were first made by Josephine, and afterward, by her and her grandson. The very last card had a little green handprint smacked in the center, decorated with tiny glitter stickers, snowflakes, ribbons, and cut-out little presents stuck to the card with, *"We Love You! Merry Christmas!"* written across the top in Josephine's beautiful hand script.

That following Christmas Eve when he noticed his mailbox was devoid of that pink envelope, he sunk into a deep, black, fathomless low that he never thought possible after reading all her past cards and letters. If *only* he continued to be in his daughter's life, maybe she wouldn't have stayed with that jerk for as long as she did. He'd have set her in the right direction again. Instead he let her continue to make her own mistakes; as a child *should* do as they were growing up. After all, how can one learn if not by making a few mistakes first? *Such was life.* But without her father's occasional guidance along the way, it looked as if she made one too many, and her world finally came crashing down around her.

Worst of all, he broke his promise to his wife.

He wasn't there when she needed a shoulder to lean on. He wasn't there to catch her when she fell. He blamed himself, but shifted all the blame back to Brian as he was snatched to the here-and-now. He watched as a single tear fell from his eye and onto the baby statue's face.

Five years had passed since that last card he got from her and his grandson. Five long years. The year he didn't get a Christmas card was the same year he went to the tavern, washed his woes away in liquor, then was struck by a car and killed, his miserly, wretched life over with--until the day he was reawakened.

He growled and faced the crowd, holding the infant statue by the neck, thrusting out towards the gaping congregation.

"**Cursed** be those Heavenly hosts!" He started. "For they have not granted me peace, but granted me this living hell, this strange punishment of having to deal with all of you--the blasphemous, the adulterous, the lecherous, the deceitful...the ***unworthy!***"

He put the statue back down and leapt on those closest to the pulpit, tearing them to shreds, as the remaining people flooded out of the church like madmen. He knocked down the candelabras, tore up poinsettias, knocked over the pews and chucked Bibles everywhere, letting out his frustrations with the world, his undead life and the loss of precious, precious days with his daughter and grandson. The only thing he didn't destroy was the nativity which held the baby in the manger.

* * *

The vampire left when he heard sirens in the distance, but the cops would never find him. They weren't capable of tracking him down.

Christmas Eve would be coming to an end soon. He figured he had caused enough mayhem to calm his already aged and fraying nerves for another year... although he still hadn't visited that vile man's girlfriend. He'd be a most unwelcome surprise at her doorstep, indeed, and he grinned in evil anticipation.

The home he arrived at was very spacious, decorated with the usual Christmas fare, including a few inflatable lawn ornaments. He decided to have a little fun and punctured an elf holding a present. He never liked elves anyway. As it deflated, he noticed a doghouse against the side of the home. Now he knew he had to keep an eye out for an animal as well.

He broke into the house through the kitchen door, his footsteps as silent as the dead. On the refrigerator were a few drawings done by a child. He kept moving through the kitchen, and into the living room, then the dining room, passing by a mantle covered in picture frames. A little boy on a tricycle, the same little boy on his first birthday, then a little older, wearing a soccer uniform with the rest of his teammates. He had a gold medal around his neck. Then one of him and his mother, her long auburn hair flowing to the side and wearing a big smile, her hazel eyes bright, her arms wrapped around her son's neck. He looked to be about 10 years old, with hair and eyes the same color as hers. There was no sign of a male figure in their lives.

The vampire paid no attention to any of the photos as he placed a dirt-encrusted, gray hand on the banister, and began making his way up the staircase to the bedrooms.

He could hear the faint tune of *"Silent Night, Holy Night"* coming from what looked like the master bedroom. It was very quiet in this home, considering it was Christmas Eve. He expected kids to still be up and about, smell of cookies baking, mugs full of cocoa and marshmallows everywhere, and a tree to be lit in the living room, with decorations plastered around. This home was as dark and as empty as his soul.

The one room, however, was lit with a warm glow. He made his way toward it and slowly poked his head in.

The woman was facing the bedroom window, looking out as

she sat in a rocking chair. This room also had its own fireplace, the flames nearly died out. A small, three foot tree was in this room, placed on a table beside the fireplace, decorated with lights, tinsel and decorations. Several small presents were under the tree, mostly all of them for her child.

Another Christmas song came from the CD player in the room, a song the vampire remembered from his own childhood, but never knew the title of. For a moment, he became still, just listening, allowing emotions he long thought dead within him to now fill him. Suddenly he felt sad for this woman, as he could feel her own sorrows emanating from her.

There was a large lump on the floor beside her feet. It lifted its head and growled towards the door. The dog. A golden retriever.

Without warning she turned, also sensing a presence in the doorway. She gasped, but the vampire didn't move. The dog growled a little louder.

"Shh. Calm down, Rocky," she told the dog. Slowly, she got up from her chair, still staring at the shadowed doorway. The vampire took a step back, further ensuring his anonymity. She tilted her head to the side, as if figuring out who it was.

"I can't *believe* this! How *dare* you step foot in here after a whole year of not a word from you! James and I *don't* need you! Not now, not *ever*, so don't think you can come crawling back here, begging for forgiveness!"

The vampire was taken aback. Her son was named James, too?

He fished through his pocket, and held the box in his hands. "Perhaps that's what he was going to do," the vampire replied, "With this trinket of deceit." He tossed it to her and she caught it.

Now *she* was looking confused. "What he was..." There was a pause. "What do you mean by that?" She tore off the wrapper, now looking at a velvet black box with gold trim. She opened it.

Inside was an engagement ring. She stared at it for a moment, then snapped the box shut, winging it back at him as hard as she could.

"*Way* too late for that, buddy," she snapped. "*Unbelievable!* **Get out**!"

"Mom?" Came a second voice from in another room.

"It's alright sweetie, just go back to sleep," she called to him.

"That's not dad... is it?" He asked.

"Brian, get out of here *now*, before I call the police," she hissed.

The vampire gasped and dropped to his knees and clasped his hands together.

"*Josephine*," he whispered.

"I mean it Brian! Get... **OUT**!"

"My Josephine..." he got up, and stepped into the room. Josephine covered her mouth and gawked at her dead father.

"My daughter... my *beloved* daughter! God had led me to you, damned wretch that I am! He still saw fit to let me find you and look at you one more time!"

Josephine was frozen in place, not sure whether to believe her eyes or not. Her father continued to speak.

"I have reflected over all the years I have lost with you, with your son. How much of a *fool* I had been after you went away with that poor excuse for a man you call Brian. All your letters... all your calls... how I ignored each and every one of them! I should have been *there* for you! I should have taken you in when you needed me *the most*! I was so stubborn and so angry, I felt as if you had abandoned me, when it was *I* who had abandoned *you*!"

All Josephine could do was slowly shake her head in absolute disbelief at what was happening right then. He continued.

"I know there's nothing I can do to change the past, and I know there's no future for us, for I am undead. My punishment for abandoning you, for leading a miserable life afterwards." He looked into her hazel eyes and paused before speaking again. "I awaken on this night every year."

Josephine lowered her hand from her mouth, the scene before her still too surreal and grisly to believe. "Dad," she whispered, taking a tiny step towards him. "Dad... is that really *you*?"

He held his hand out to her. Ever so slowly, she put her warm hand in his taloned, icy one.

"I... I saw you *buried*. I saw you put into the *ground*. I saw them put dirt on your *grave*..."

"And yet I still walk once a year, cursed because of my imprudent ways."

James stepped into the room, and let out a loud gasp. Josephine and her father pulled away, looking at him.

"*You...*" the vampire started, staring into another pair of hazel eyes.

The *same eyes* he peered into at the bistro.

"It's the *Angel of Death*, mom! The one I told you I saw!" He ran to the fireplace and grabbed a poker, swinging it wildly at the vampire. "You stay away from my mom! You're not gonna kill her too!"

Josephine gasped at her father. "You... *you're* the one James told me about? The one who killed everyone in the bistro? But... but *why*?"

James looked at his mom, confused. "You *know* him?"

Josephine was now stuck in a tight situation. She found it amazing she was able to calm her son down after he came home screaming hysterically about some Angel of Death killing everyone in the bistro, but *this...*

"James, this--this is your *grandfather.*" She tightened her grip on her son's shoulders.

James lowered the poker, still gawking at the tattered, filthy, undead creature before him. "Grandpa's an Angel of Death?" He looked at his mom in awe. "Are we angels too?"

"We all belong to God, sweetie. But your grandfather here is no angel."

The vampire dropped to his knees again so he could get a closer look at his grandson, tears coming from his red eyes. "James.... James...." he kept whispering to himself, then swept him up in an embrace. "I'm so sorry, dear boy....I'm so, *so sorry....*"

James tried not to grimace at the stench emanating from his long dead grandfather. But then he stood up, smiling at Josephine with pointed teeth.

"You've raised him so well on your own. I just wish I had been there to *help* you."

"Just having you tell me that is enough," she replied.

Gently, the vampire touched his daughter's face, and she did her best not to flinch at his icy touch.

"Please release me, Josephine. Only you can do it. I'm tired.

So, very, *very* tired. I have come to terms with my past, and I see your future will be without further worries. I need not haunt this world, or your life, anymore."

She gave her father one last hug, despite the dried blood all over his coat. "I love you, Daddy."

* * *

Josephine led him up to her attic, and sat a chair in the middle of the room, in front of a window that faced East. They talked long into the wee hours of the morning.

"I can't believe you were *that* angry at me," Josephine said. "All that time. Sometimes, I was sad at your non-replies, and sometimes I was angry. I just couldn't figure out what I had done to make you so mad at me."

The vampire sighed. "I realize it wasn't you I was angry at... it was the fact you had grown up, and had to live your own life. I wanted you to stay my little girl forever. My foolish pride was what stopped me from going to you when you needed help," he sighed. "I just wish you had found a better man to share your life with."

"It took me a long time to learn my lesson, but one thing's for sure, I'm definitely *not* in a rush to find another," she replied. "James is all I need."

He paused. "Just... *remember* this ordeal, please. I wouldn't want you following in my footsteps once James gets to be at that certain age when he wants to... leave the nest."

Josephine gave a tiny grin. "I think I have it covered."

Despite their long talk, he never confessed to having killed Brian. She'd hear about it on the news soon enough, and he'd be long gone.

The sky was a dull pink. The sun would be rising soon. Father and daughter looked at each other. Even under the black-veined, pasty pallor and red eyes, she still saw the father she knew and remembered.

"Merry Christmas, Daddy," she whispered as they held hands.

"Merry Christmas, Sweetheart."

They embraced one more time before she rushed to the attic entrance, holding back her sobs as she closed the door.

32

The vampire sighed once more, and took out the photo of his daughter and grandson, both with bright smiles. Josephine came out strong in the end. That's all that mattered. And that gave him the sweet serenity and peace he yearned for during his undead years.

He stayed transfixed on their picture as the first rays of light pierced the sky, the warm, golden-orange glow filling the attic as he burst into flames, still smiling as he stared into the eyes of his beloved daughter.

It was the best Christmas present he had ever received.

Story Art Cover
By David Naughton-Shires
http://www.TheImageDesigns.com

Dedication
To Andrew. See you under the mistletoe.

Author Bio
Melissa Helwig is a Print Journalism graduate who currently lives in Oakville, Ontario. She has been a fan of the horror genre for as long as she can remember. She is the creator of blog Little Miss Zombie (http://www.littlemisszombie.blogspot.com), where she reviews horror books and movies.

All I Want for Christmas is Stu
By Melissa Helwig

5 Days until Christmas

Sheila looked around the cafeteria and was impressed by the Christmas decorations. This didn't look like the room where she ate her bologna and cheese sandwich every day at noon. This was a magical winter wonderland. Fake snow was everywhere. Each table was covered with a red tablecloth. Tinsel hung from the ceiling, along with a banner that said "Merry Christmas to the Staff at H&H". A huge Christmas tree, decorated beautifully, was at the front of the room. Even mistletoe and stockings were hung.

Sheila had worked at Harrod & Hanley Foods for ten years and this was the first time she had ever attended the Christmas party. She had always found being at the factory from 7:00 a.m. – 3:00 p.m. was bad enough. She didn't want to waste a Saturday night there too.

Her job at H&H was hard work. At the factory they made turkeys. Or rather, they made them ready for consumption. Killed them, gutted them, removed the feathers (and other unwanted body parts), stuffed them with dressing made at the factory and shipped them off to grocery stores ready for your freezer.

Sheila had the unpleasant job of removing the gizzards from the turkeys. It wasn't too bad, since the turkeys were basically bloodless hunks of meat by the time they reached her, but the gizzards still had a repulsive, squishy feel to them.

By Saturday, Sheila was usually too tired to do anything, and spent her weekends watching television with her two children, Robbie, age 10, and Cindy, age 8.

But not this year. This year she had lost twenty-five pounds and was now a size 14. She hadn't been less than two hundred pounds in 20 years. She felt beautiful and confident, and ready to find a new man.

Her ex-husband had left her eight years ago when he revealed that he was gay. Shelia was shocked and devastated. Their love life was just fine. They had two children for God's

37

sake! She was convinced she had done something to turn him off women.

As a result, she never even tried to date. There must be something seriously wrong with her to change a perfectly straight man into a homosexual.

But now, at age forty, Sheila realized she didn't want to spend the rest of her life alone. Also, there was a guy at work that she was interested in...and maybe – just maybe – he could be interested in her too.

His name was Stu and they constantly flirted. She would giggle at his corny jokes; he would softly touch her shoulder or arm while chatting. They would whisper gossip about others, Sheila loving the way Stu's warm breath felt on her ear and neck.

But Stu was mysterious. He rarely talked about himself and dodged any questions Sheila would ask him. She knew very little about him. She had no clue where he lived, if he had a family or pets, even his exact age.

Plus, he had recently switched to the night shift and now Sheila never saw him anymore.

So she had her fingers crossed that he would be at the Christmas party tonight and get the chance to give him her number. She wore a sexy little black dress with a tiny wreath brooch pinned to her chest; she didn't want anyone to accuse her of not being festive.

She took a seat at the table near the Christmas tree and anxiously waited for Stu to arrive.

* * *

Two hours later, everyone was finished with their dinner – turkey with cranberry sauce, stuffing, mashed potatoes with gravy, turnip, a dinner roll and pumpkin pie for dessert – and Stu still hadn't shown up.

Sheila had given up. She didn't need a man to have fun. She was on her fourth glass of red wine and feeling a bit tipsy and happily chatting away to her co-workers when Stu strolled in.

She was so startled she knocked her wine glass over and it spilled onto her lap.

38

All I Want For Christmas is Stu

"Oops! I'm such a klutz!" Sheila giggled, her face turning as red as the tablecloth.

"Whoa, someone's had too much to drink!" Tom, a loud-mouth who Sheila despised, shouted.

"Excuse me," she said, standing up from the table.

On the way to the washroom, Stu caught her eye and grinned.

When she stepped out of the washroom he was waiting for her.

"Hey, Sheila. You look great!"

"Thanks," she said, blushing. "It feels like I haven't seen you in forever!"

"I know. It's been awhile. Come here, I got you a Christmas present," he smiled, grabbing her hand and pulling her to the corner of the room.

He handed her a small box wrapped in shiny green paper, tied with a lacy red bow.

She opened it and inside was a pair of leather gloves.

"Because you lost yours a few weeks ago."

"You remembered?" Sheila gasped.

He nodded.

"Thank you!"

Then Stu leaned in and kissed her.

It was as good as Sheila had imagined.

His lips were soft and warm, his breath minty. Their tongues collided and swirled around each other. Then he pulled away and kissed her cheek, slowly trailing down to her neck. First he kissed her softly, then harder, sucking on her neck, his warm breath feeling so good. Next he nibbled on her neck. Gently, at first, then harder. She felt both pain and pleasure simultaneously. Exquisite pain.

She was so immersed in that feeling that she didn't see her co-worker, Carl, approach until he stood directly in front of them.

Stu stopped and looked up.

"Hey, Carl," said Sheila.

He didn't respond. He simply pulled a shotgun out from under his coat and shot Stu in the face. The wall behind him was painted a festive red and chunks of bone from his skull fell like snowflakes.

Shelia screamed. Everybody screamed.

Then Carl calmly walked over to their boss, Randy, and shot him in the head. He stumbled backward into the Christmas tree, which subsequently fell over, sending Christmas ornaments flying across the room.

The angel fell at Carl's feet. He crushed it as he moved forward to shoot Tom. This time Carl's aim was off and he shot him in the chest. Tom fell backwards onto a table, knocking several wine glasses over in the process. Carl didn't think a shot in the chest was good enough, so he stepped closer and shot him again in the belly and the head. Red wine and blood flowed off the table, like a red waterfall.

Someone must have called the cops at the first gunshot because they showed up then, telling Tom to drop the weapon and put his hands on his head. He did what they asked.

They handcuffed him and led him out of the room.

Another officer helped the others out of the room, making sure everyone else was all right.

Some cried, upset over the deaths of Stu, Randy and Tom. But most just felt relived that it wasn't them being carried away in a body bag.

Shelia was one of the former. She couldn't believe she had come this close to her dream of being with Stu, only to have it taken away.

She wiped blood off her neck. She didn't know if it was hers or Stu's.

4 Days Until Christmas

"I brought a tray of Christmas cookies for you, but they wouldn't let me bring it in," Sheila said.

"That's okay," Carl replied. "You know, you're my first visitor. Probably will be my only one, too."

"Yeah, well. We were good friends, Carl. You're a good guy."

"I suppose."

"Why did you do it? How could you do such a thing? Stu and Randy and Tom are *dead*," she said, tears forming in her eyes.

"I'll tell you the same thing I told all of them. They were monsters."

"*What?* Stu was one of the nicest guys you could ever meet – "

"No, you don't understand. They were monsters, as in creatures who feed off the blood of humans."

Sheila didn't know what to say. She was stunned. He was insane. He was making up excuses for killing three men because he didn't have a reason. He was a psychopath. That's all there was to it.

"No. They weren't monsters. You're the monster. I think we're done here," Sheila said, standing up to leave.

"You should be thanking me! I saved all of your lives!" He shouted as Sheila left.

Sheila couldn't believe what Carl said to her. What a psycho. Monsters. If he honestly believed that, he needed serious help.

On the drive home Sheila was parched. She went through the McDonald's drive-through and ordered a large Diet Coke. It didn't quench her thirst.

3 Days Until Christmas

Stu had left one hell of a hickey. There were two teeth marks on her neck, surrounded by a swollen red patch. It hurt a lot. She cleaned it with peroxide, applied Polysporin and put a huge bandage on it.

She heard a scream from outside and then heard the door opening.

"Mommy!" Cindy wailed. "I-fell-off-my-sled!"

Sheila ran down the stairs to her daughter.

"Aw, let me see it, sweetheart."

There was a hole worn in the knee of her purple snowsuit and she had skinned her knee.

"It doesn't look too bad," Sheila tried to soothe her.

"Here, let's go clean it up," she said grabbing her hand and leading her upstairs.

She lifted Cindy onto the bathroom counter.

"Do you want me to kiss it better?"

Cindy nodded.

Sheila leaned down and kissed her knee. She could taste the blood on her lips. It didn't taste metallic like it usually did.

It tasted delicious, like her favorite wine.

She licked the wound and tasted more blood on her tongue. She needed more. She couldn't help herself. She sucked the wound. Hard. Felt warm blood trickle into her mouth and slide down her throat, filling her belly. Her thirst finally felt like it was being quenched.

"Ow! Mommy that hurts!"

As soon as she heard Cindy's voice, she pulled away, ashamed.

She was a monster. She was beginning to understand – and believe.

2 Days Until Christmas

The deaths of her co-workers had been a wild way to start her Christmas vacation. But life still had to go on. She had two kids who had sent Santa Claus very long letters. So she went out to Wal-Mart to pick up a few last-minute gifts.

Sheila could only get her mother to babysit at night, so she arrived home late.

She was getting her parcels out of her trunk when she felt someone step up behind her.

"Boo!" He said.

Sheila jumped, spun around and promptly dropped the bag in her hand, along with her jaw.

It was Stu.

"Sorry. Here. I'll get those," he said, bending down to pick up the bags.

Sheila felt light-headed and thought she might faint.

"...I must be imagining this...you're dead."

"Nope. They thought so, but I'm fine. If I wasn't, how could I be standing here with you?"

"Um, I saw your fucking brains explode all over the wall!" Sheila yelled, becoming frantic.

How could this be? He died right before her eyes.

"Um...do you want to come in?" Sheila asked.

She didn't know what else to say. She was happy to see him, but knew it was impossible. And that frightened her a little.

"Sure. I'll help you with your bags."

Once they were inside, Sheila put the presents in her secret hiding spot (her bedroom closet, very original) and they sat at the kitchen table, waiting for the coffee to brew.

"Oh, did I do that to your neck?" Stu winced. "I'm sorry."

"Don't worry about it. It's fine."

"I'm ready to continue if you are," he said, holding her hand and leaning in for a kiss.

Sheila turned her head.

"Look, I think you should go."

"What? But what about my coffee?"

"I'm really busy. There's only two days left until Christmas. I have presents to wrap, cookies to bake, cards to write. I'm really sorry. Maybe after Christmas?"

Stu grinned. "Yeah, sure."

"You're welcome here anytime after Christmas, I'll be free then."

That made Stu grin even wider.

1 Day Until Christmas

It was Christmas Eve. Sheila's kids were watching *How The Grinch Stole Christmas* while her mother snored on the couch beside them. She was on her computer reading about vampires on Wikipedia.

If Carl was telling the truth and Stu, Randy and Tom were vampires, he made a big mistake by shooting them. Apparently it was common knowledge that vampires could only be killed with a wooden stake.

Sheila didn't know since she never watched horror movies; too scary for her. She preferred a nice romantic comedy, something with Sandra Bullock or Julia Roberts. Maybe so did Carl and that's why he didn't know. In any case, he made a grave error by using a shotgun. Since vampires are already dead, they can't be killed – except with a wooden stake.

That explains why Stu was still alive. Randy and Tom were probably still kicking too.

She also made a mistake inviting Stu into her home. Once you invite a vampire into your home, they're free to come and go as they please. That's why Stu kept grinning yesterday. He probably planned on finishing her off.

Melissa Helwig

But she had a plan to save Stu and herself.

If you kill the head vampire, then the rest of the clan reverts back to normal. And she had an inkling who the head vampire was.

Randy was the boss at work, so it would make sense for him to be the boss of the vampires. He probably had a plot to turn all H&H employees into vampires...or something.

She gathered her equipment, (a wooden stake and some garlic), took one last look at her kids, and left for her boss's house.

He lived in a large house on the opposite side of town as her.

When she arrived, she realized she had no idea what to do.

She decided to sneak up to the house and peek in the window to see if he was actually still alive. All she saw was his wife sitting alone on the couch. Then Sheila realized she was talking to someone. She could hear a voice, she just needed to see him to be sure it was him.

Bingo! There was Randy standing right in the window...staring right back at her.

Sheila gasped and ducked down, but knew it was too late. A light shone on her from the porch and she knew it was too late.

"Sheila, is that you?" Randy asked, squinting into the dark. "What are you doing here at this hour?"

He didn't sound mad, he simply sounded curious.

She held the stake behind her back and walked towards him.

"Oh, I, uh, just wanted to wish you a Merry Christmas." It was a horrible lie and Sheila kicked herself, but it was the only thing she could think of.

"Well, Merry Christmas to you too Sheila."

He was only standing a foot away from her and she realized that it was now or never. She lunged forward, stake in hand, and plunged it directly into his heart.

Randy just stared at her and for a second she thought Wikipedia was wrong (of course an encyclopedia which *anyone* can edit would be wrong). When suddenly he shriveled up like a prune, then his skin melted and he was just a skeleton, and the skeleton turned to dust.

Sheila smiled. She saved Stu and herself!

44

When she got home she felt joyful. She wouldn't become a bloodsucking member of the undead after all! She raced into her house to give her children great big hugs and kisses.

"Robbie, Cindy, I –"

When she stepped into the living room she stopped dead in her tracks.

Her mom was pale as ghost and had blood dripping from her neck. Same with Robbie.

But Cindy didn't. What was happening to Cindy was much worse. She was sitting on Stu's lap. His mouth was pressed to her neck and was sucking her blood through the two holes he had punctured. Stu was sucking her neck fast and hard, like he was sucking on an extra thick milkshake and couldn't seem to get any liquid through the straw. But he wasn't having any difficulty sucking any of Cindy's vital fluids. Sheila could tell by her pale skin and blue lips. She was practically sucked dry.

Sheila felt defeated. Randy wasn't the head vampire. But then she realized she didn't care anymore. All she wanted was revenge for what this monster did to her family.

He hadn't noticed her presence or even heard her call out to her kids because he was too preoccupied with feeding off her daughter like a spider feeds off a fly.

The thought of it made her ill and angry.

The stake was still in her coat pocket. She grasped it in her sweaty palm and leapt at Stu, aiming for his heart. She missed, stabbing the couch arm instead.

Stu knocked her onto the floor.

"You thought you could kill me? Don't make me laugh. Thanks for the feast, by the way. I haven't eaten like this in years. It was a perfect holiday meal. I was planning on making you my bride, but I can't really trust a woman who tried to kill me now, can I? I guess I'll just have to drink your blood too."

He knelt on the floor beside her and kissed her.

"For old time's sake."

Then he moved his mouth to her neck, sunk his teeth in and bit into a clove of garlic.

He fell onto his back, gagging and struggling to breathe.

Sheila grabbed the stake off the floor and knelt over him. This time she wouldn't miss. She drove the stake into his chest over and over until he was nothing but a pile of dust, just like

Randy.

"Mom, what happened?" Robbie asked groggily.

Cindy and Sheila's mother started at her with confused expressions on their faces.

"Stu must've been the head vampire," she muttered.

"What?" They said in unison.

"Nothing!" She replied cheerfully. "We better get to bed or Santa won't come!"

The kids excitedly raced to bed, Sheila and her mother not far behind.

Christmas Day

Everything was back to normal. No more vampires. No more bite marks on their necks. It was simply a wonderful snowy Christmas day filled with presents, food and time spent with family.

Sheila thought perhaps she would be better off without a man in her life.

MISTLETOE, CROSSES, & VAMPIRES

BY SUZANNE ROBB

Story Art Cover
By Ian Kobe
www.squidsicle.com

Dedication
To Ian, closer than blood to me.

Author Bio
Suzanne Robb's debut novel Z-Boat will be released
by Twisted Library Press. She has stories in several anthologies currently out and soon to be released. In her free time she reads, watches
movies, plays with her dog, and enjoys chocolate and Legos. To learn
more check out http://www.suzannerobb.blogspot.com/

Mistletoe, Crosses, and Vampires
Suzanne Robb

Ivan tossed the blood bag to the side. He wiped a hand across his face to clear off any residue left on his lips. He looked at his hand, a few crimson red droplets smeared across it. He brought his hand up to his nose and inhaled deeply, then snaked his tongue out to lick them off.

Cassandra walked up to him, looked at the blood bag then shook her head.

"You know you can't just leave bodies lying around, it draws suspicion. The last thing we want is a damn bounty hunter after us." Cassandra leaned in close to Ivan and licked his chin.

"I know, don't worry." Ivan shivered as he felt her tongue on his neck gradually move up to his chin.

"You missed a spot." Cassandra smiled as she pulled away.

Ivan gave her a smile, then walked over to the body and picked it up. A gutter grate exited into a canal at the end of the alley, he would dispose of the body there. As he walked Cassandra followed.

An observer would see an average couple, perhaps a bit paler than normal, but not unusual for this time of year. The male stood about six foot tall with short blond hair and a lanky build. The female had a shorter more athletic figure and long curly brown hair. If one were to look in their eyes too long they might notice something off, something different, something evil.

"I hate this time of year, they've ruined solstice." Cassandra pouted for a few seconds then grabbed Ivan's hand.

Ivan looked down at the small cool hand in his. He thought about how long they had known each other, and how much he loved her. They had been together for over two hundred years, and he had yet to tire of her.

"You always say that, but when you get your present you always change your mind." Ivan readjusted the body so Cassandra could lean into him.

"I suppose, but I don't think you can top last year. You really outdid yourself with a monastery, all that innocent virgin blood. I was bloated for a week, but it was well worth it, especially the way you decorated the tree with intestinal garlands and eyeball ornaments when we were done."

Ivan smiled at the memory, he really had outdone himself. This year would have to be something really special, something to celebrate their two hundred years of slaughtering.

When they reached the end of the alley he kicked up the grate with his foot and dropped the body inside of it. In a few days nothing but a water logged corpse would be found, half eaten by rats.

"Now you've gone and made me hungry. I'm going to go find some fast food, in the mood for a run." Leaning up Cassandra gave Ivan a peck on the cheek then left.

Ivan smiled at his luck. When he turned her he didn't know she would be so perfect for him. The process changed the personality of the human, but her humor, smile, and ability to maim and torture mirrored him in so many ways.

As Ivan walked down the street he sensed someone watching him, but couldn't find the source. He tightened his coat around him, more of an unconscious gesture than any real need to fight off the cold. They were being watched.

* * *

Derek put down the binoculars and hid behind the wall. He had been following the trail of these two vampires for the last six months. The time to get them neared, he couldn't waste much more time with surveillance or they would discover him, tonight had been close.

He knelt down and packed up his bag, time to go back to the warehouse and come up with a plan. He threw the bag over his shoulder, pulled on a beanie, sunglasses, and earphones. Within seconds Derek looked like any other guy walking down the crowded street looking for Christmas gifts.

The holiday crowd thick with shoppers, bags, and pick pockets. Derek felt the little hand, the second it reached for his wallet. He grabbed it shocking the thief.

"You shouldn't steal kid, you never know what might happen."

The boy looked up at him, blue eyes set in a dirty face. He

couldn't have been more than twelve.

"I'm sorry mister, I swear I won't ever do it again." The boy tried to pull his hand away, but Derek held tight to it.

"Where are your parents?"

The boy broke eye contact and started to wiggle out of Derek's grip. Derek tightened his hold and led the boy over to the side near an alley entrance. The boys eyes widened in fear.

"Look, I'm not going to hurt you. I just want to know where your parents are. From the looks of you, I'd say you don't have any, then again parenting isn't regulated very well in places like this."

"My parents are dead okay? I had a foster family, but living with them is worse than living out here. Now let go of me or I'll scream."

Derek looked into eyes far too old for the young body they were in. He made an impulsive decision, not something he usually did.

"Let me help you. The streets aren't a place for a kid your age."

The boy laughed. "I've heard that before, I'm not interested."

Derek leaned down so he was eye level with the kid. "Not like that, just let me help you. Let's start with dinner. You like cheeseburgers?"

"Okay, but you're buying."

Derek let go of the kid and laughed. He caught himself and looked down at the scamp who had tried to take his wallet. When was the last time he laughed? He shook off the dismal thought and led the boy to a diner near the warehouse where he lived.

Derek made sure to sit in the booth with a clear view of all entry points. He ordered food for both of them, and a soda for the boy.

"What's your name?"

The boy took a large sip of his soda before answering. "Calvin."

"That's a good name, I'm Derek." Calvin looked at him and tilted his head to the side.

"What do you do Derek? You don't look like a business man, and you're too old to be a student."

Derek choked on his coffee. How long had it been since he

had talked with someone so blatantly honest?

"I guess the best name for what I do is bounty hunting." Calvin's eyes lit up.

"Really, do you get to carry a gun? Have you ever killed anyone? Have you gotten beat up?"

Derek held up a hand. "Whoa kid, slow down. I'm old remember, can't keep up with light speed."

Derek had no idea how to answer. He had killed lots, but not people. He had never killed a human. Vampires were monsters so killing them didn't really count. As for being beat up, he had the crap kicked out of him multiple times. He had the scars to prove it.

"I do sometimes carry a gun. I've been in a fight or two. I've never, and I mean never, killed another human being."

Calvin slumped in his seat. Derek noticed he seemed let down. Oh well, not his problem. Movies always made his profession seem cooler than reality.

"Are you good at what you do?" Calvin sat up as the food arrived.

Derek thought about it, he was alive that meant something. "Yes, I'm very good at what I do. Now eat up."

Calvin inhaled his cheeseburger and Derek watching in amusement. He wondered when the last time the kid had an actual meal. Situations like this made him angry. Homeless kids and orphaned kids were a grim reality, yet outside people were worried about whether or not they had everything on their gift list, or if they had enough stamps for Christmas cards.

"You want some dessert?" The light in Calvin's eyes, all he needed.

Derek motioned to the waitress, Dez. "Hey Dez, can you get some pie and ice cream for my friend here?"

The waitress looked at Calvin and smiled. "Sure thing, what kind of ice cream you want kid"

"Um, strawberry and chocolate."

"You got it." Desiree winked and walked away.

Derek watched as she left. He had flirted with her for a few months now, but nothing had come of it. Now all of a sudden she winked at him. Women were not able to resist the lure of a man with a kid, it had to be Calvin.

"Aren't you having dessert?"

"No, just some more coffee."

A moment later a huge slice of pie with two oversized scoops of ice cream appeared in front of Calvin.

"Don't eat too fast or you'll get sick."

Calvin just nodded his head as he dug in.

"This your son?" Derek looked like a deer in headlights.

"No, he's more like a nephew, looking after him for a bit."

"Well I got two of my own, about the same age. Let me know if you need any help."

Derek nodded as Dez left. Well there went that. He had a strict policy about dating women with kids. He didn't do it, not that he had anything against kids, he just couldn't risk putting them in danger.

Calvin was different. Derek knew he would be safer with him than he would be on the streets. Drug dealers, pimps, and other things could prey on him. He smiled as the kid had almost finished his pie. All Derek had to do was convince Calvin to come back to the warehouse without coming off a weirdo.

"Calvin, why don't you stay at my place tonight? See if you like it. You'll get your own room, and lots of space because it's a warehouse –"

"You live in a warehouse? That is the coolest thing ever." Calvin shot out of his seat ready to go.

Derek stood and threw money on the table. As he walked out with Calvin he nodded at Desiree.

"I have one rule though, and you have to obey it at all times."

"Okay, but nothing weird or I'm leaving."

Derek shook his head. "No it's nothing weird. There's a workroom, it's off limits. No matter what, you don't go in that room, understood?"

Calvin stopped and looked at him. "You don't do anything weird in that room do you?"

Derek shook his head.

"Okay I can agree to that."

"Good then, tomorrow we'll get you some clean clothes. For tonight I'll scrounge up something for you."

* * *

Cassandra came back to the house covered in blood. Ivan smelled her immediately. He sped to her licking the warm blood off every crevice of her body. She knew how to drive him mad with need. He had already fed, but his appetite had been renewed.

"Damn it, the sun's going to be up soon, can't go and feed."

Cassandra smiled evilly. "Wait here a minute."

Ivan watched her walk to the door and open it. She reached out an arm for something, a second later she dragged in a limp body.

"I brought some dessert just in case. We'll have to wait for him to wake up before we can have any fun."

Ivan smiled and once again wrapped himself around her. This time they were kissing, their hands all over one another. Ivan had several ideas about what to do in order to pass the time.

The next night Ivan awoke with a pleasurable sensation in his stomach. He loved waking up full, it took the pressure off of having to hunt. He rolled out of bed and looked at the decaying corpse in the corner. He had forgotten the name of the guy, but he had tasted good, and had a nice house.

Going to the closet Ivan grabbed a clean shirt and pair of jeans. The prior resident, a clothes hog with good taste. Poor Cassandra had to go out and get her clothes, though she didn't mind shopping, or stealing.

Dressed and ready to start the night Ivan began to mentally plan his Solstice surprise. He had a fairly good idea what to do this year. When he went out the other day he had seen a flyer for some orphanage putting on a recital to raise funds.

Ivan reached far back into his memory banks certain he had never done an orphanage before. Cassandra loved kids, so this would be one of the best gifts he could give her. He just needed to make sure to seal the exits, cut off cell phone use, and take care of the alarm system.

"What are you doing honey? Thought you would be exhausted after last night?"

Ivan turned to look at his love. Cassandra stood there naked, smears of blood all over her body. "Satiated yes, but energized. I'm off to make preparations, you know the deal. Don't follow me, I don't want you to ruin the surprise."

"You won't top last year."

Ivan just smiled as he left. He knew she would spend some time with their dessert before hunting for a real meal.

Ivan on the other hand had to make sure they were safe. The perfect gift was important, but making sure they were not being followed was more important. The last several days he kept feeling eyes on him, but could never see anyone.

Either they were very good at what they did, or his age finally made him paranoid. Stranger things had been known to happen, vampires going crazy after living too long. He had been around for seven hundred years, it wasn't impossible. He could be starting to lose it.

Ivan walked down the street, same as he had done the past few days and waited for the sensation. After a few blocks he felt it. He slowed his pace and began to look in various windows pretending to look at the displays.

He looked in all the shadowy locations using the glass windows a mirror. He saw nothing out of the ordinary, then in an alley a man watching him. As soon as he spotted him the man knelt down, out of view.

He spun around and crossed the street in seconds. He found the man shoving a pair of binoculars into a bag. Ivan reached down and grabbed the man by the neck.

"Who are you? Why are you watching me?"

"Derek, my name is Derek. I have no idea who the hell you are. If you want money take my wallet, just don't hurt me."

The man seemed to be genuinely scared. Bounty hunters were usually more macho, and a lot more careful. Ivan didn't release his grip, with his other hand he reached for the man's wallet. Looking at the ID, it confirmed the man's name, no license to carry a weapon, no police ID

Ivan placed the man on the ground. He snatched the binoculars out of the bag and held them up in front of the perspiring man.

"What are these for? I saw you watching me?"

"I swear I wasn't watching you, I'm making sure they work. I got them for my nephew and wanted to make sure they were good."

Ivan raised an eyebrow. "Really, and what need does your nephew have for something like this?"

"He likes to go hiking, thought he could use them. Safety first you know?"

Ivan listened to the man's heartbeat, it raced inside his rib-cage. He perspired even though it was cold out for human standards. Ivan broke the binoculars against the wall and waked away. He had to be getting paranoid, about to attack a man in public over a stupid gift.

Ivan headed towards the orphanage, with Solstice only a few days away he needed to arrange the surprise before he went crazy.

* * *

Derek fell against the wall and let out a breath. His heart pounding, sweat dripping off of him liberally. If Calvin had come out and seen that, if the vampire had not believed his lies the boy would be dead.

He had been so careful, he had wanted to take them out to-night, kill them and be done with it. The problem with that plan, he hadn't found where they lived. The male was too smart and waited until the last minute to run home, Derek could never keep up.

Over the last two weeks he had grown fond of Calvin, he could never live with himself if something happened to him. He looked down at the broken binoculars and sighed. He had to kill these vampires, he knew who they were and what they would do soon.

In the bounty hunter circle they were known as the Christmas Terrors. For the last two hundred years they could be traced back to the most heinous crimes, all of which occurred on Christmas Eve. Derek had to act fast, or else there would be another massacre in two days.

"Hey what happened to your binoculars? Why do you ha-"

"Calvin, let's go get something to eat, I bet you're hungry."

Derek grabbed his bag and led the way to a coffee shop down the street. He knew this area well. He grew up down the street in the orphanage. He thought back to those days. They were some of the worst of his life.

His parents had died in a car accident leaving him all alone. No family came forward, so from the ages of seven to eighteen he belonged to the state. No one adopted older kids, or fostered them. Derek developed anger issues, and soon became known as a problem child.

The day he turned eighteen Derek left the orphanage and never looked back. He proceeded to get into several fights, get arrested multiple times, and create a name for himself as a member of the 'wrong crowd.'

One night he picked a fight with a guy twice his size and won. Derek managed to stumble out of the bar before the police showed. In the alleyway he met some guy who helped him back to his place. When Derek woke the next morning the guy sat there, watching him.

That day Derek's life changed forever. The man, a vampire hunter, told Derek his story. He laughed at first, but later, the man had proven his seriousness when he took Derek out on the hunt.

From that night on he had been his apprentice, learning everything he could. That had been twenty years ago. His mentor, Kyle, retired a few years back so now it was just Derek. He had adjusted to the silence over time, but surprised himself at how quickly he adapted to the noise of a twelve year old running around.

Looking across the table at the boy Derek thought about what he had to do. He needed to protect him, and figure out where the vampire couple were going to strike on Christmas. He had been following the male for months and still had no idea.

Derek had less than two days to find out what they had planned or a lot of people were going to die. He looked around the café and outside the window he saw the male vampire walking down the street.

What the hell would he be doing down there? Not much selection when it came to feeding, no stores, only a school, a local park, library, and the orphanage.

"Oh God." Derek felt sick to his stomach.

"What's wrong, is the food bad?" Calvin looked around with a worried expression on his face.

"No, food's fine. Are you done? I need to do some work."

Calvin nodded his head. Derek stood, tossed too much cash on the table and left in a hurry. He needed to get to the warehouse and start prepping. He knew the building they were going to attack like the back of his hand, but going up against two old vampires with kids and freaked out parents would make things difficult.

He thought about calling in a bomb threat or something so they would cancel the yearly Christmas Eve recital, but knew they would just choose another location, one Derek might not find out about in time.

Back in the warehouse Derek set Calvin up with some movies and a soda.

"Stay here, don't go out tonight. I'm going to be in my office."

"Okay."

Derek walked over to the door and opened it with his key card. Inside, the most advanced weaponry developed to fight vampires. There were guns with wood tipped bullets, grenades full of holy water, crosses, wooden stakes, crossbows, and everything else you could think of.

As he looked over the weapons, he had to be very careful with his selection. Grenades were out, so were crossbows, and guns, too much risk of a bystander getting hurt with those. That left him with the traditional weapons.

He prepared a bag with holy water vials, crosses, wooden stakes, and some communion wafers. He had a plan brewing in his head and hoped it worked.

* * *

Ivan had taken care of the alarm, and cut the hard lines for the phone. There were only two exits to worry about, not a problem. The only thing left to do, figure out a way to deal with cell phones. As of late they had become a hindrance to his kind.

Everywhere he looked someone was using one of those damn things to call the police, take a picture, or upload a video. He hated them with a passion.

A familiar scent distracted him, type O negative, his favorite. Ivan searched the area around him until he found the source, a woman in her mid-twenties, brunette, running alone on the park path. How he loved women who thought running at night was safe. Using his natural speed and grace he ran up to the woman.

"Excuse me, I need to tell you something."

"Leave me alone you creep." She sped up.

Ivan easily matched her pace. "You smell delicious."

The woman looked at Ivan then screamed as he let his fangs out and dragged her off the path and into the bushes. She fought and kicked which only drove his need to feed. He tore into her neck ripping the carotid artery. The spray of blood drove his hunger wild, a moment later she stopped fighting him and went limp. He feasted on her, enjoying every last warm drop. When the blood got cold he stopped drinking, that was the rule.

Standing up he felt better. He wasn't going crazy, he just needed to eat, and the pressure of finding the perfect gift for Cassandra must be getting to him. Which reminded him, he better get home before she got curious and decided to track his scent. He didn't want her ruining the surprise.

He walked into the house smiling as Cassandra walked up to him. She grabbed him by the hand and led him to the bathroom. There were several candles lit and cool bath had been drawn.

"Hey handsome, want to help me wash my back?"

"Of course my lady, your wish is my command."

Ivan watched as Cassandra slipped into the water. He stripped out of his own clothes, letting them drop in a bloody heap next to the trash can. He grabbed a wash cloth soaping it up. Cassandra leaned forward and he began to clean her back in small rhythmic motions.

"Happy birthday love. Your present is all picked out."

Cassandra turned to look at him. She smiled, but then a pensive look crossed her face.

"What's wrong, you look tired." Cassandra reached out a hand a caressed his cheek.

Ivan tried to smile reassuringly. "Nothing to worry about, just getting old." He laughed to try and make light of it.

Cassandra looked forward but Ivan knew the look of worry was still there. The only thing that would remove it would be her present. Thankfully it was only two days away.

* * *

Derek was making pancakes when Calvin came into the kitchen. He wiped sleep out of his eyes and brightened at the sight of food.

"Here you go kid, maple syrup is on the table." Calvin grabbed the plate and sat at the table.

Derek sat next to him and poured them both of them a glass of orange juice.

"Calvin, I need to go out for a bit tonight. I want you to stay here until I get back okay?"

Calvin looked up at Derek. "But it's Christmas Eve, can't you go out another time?"

"I'm sorry kiddo, it has to be tonight, but it won't be for long I promise."

"Is it a work thing?"

Derek shoved a mouth full of pancake into his mouth as he thought how to answer. Honesty was best.

"Yeah it is."

Calvin didn't respond and Derek felt the weight of disappointment settle onto his shoulders. At least he had some presents for the kid to open on Christmas. He had no idea how long it had been since Calvin had a real Christmas.

Derek looked at his watch, thirty minutes until sunset. He sat in his office thinking about what he had to do. There were going to be a lot of innocent bystanders. He could warn them, but last time he did that people called him crazy. Until people saw, they wouldn't believe. He hoped he could at least get most of them out alive.

He grabbed the bolt cutters off the wall and threw them in his bag. He knew the vampire would use chains to lock the exits. The alarm would be taken care of, as well as the phones.

Derek hefted his bag onto his shoulder, as a last thought he grabbed one of the guns. He had a feeling he would need it.

'Better safe than sorry.'

When he came out of the room he ran into Calvin.

"Hey, what are you up to?"

"I'm just making some popcorn then watching a movie." Calvin hit the start button on the microwave.

"Good, sounds like fun. I'll see you later, don't wait up."

* * *

Ivan and Cassandra were out the door as soon as the sun went down. Ivan had blindfolded Cassandra so the surprise would not be ruined. He led her as fast as he could to the orphanage. For his plan to work he had to do a few things, and only had moments to do them.

He stopped outside of the building, putting his hands on Cassandra's shoulders.

"Wait here."

"Yes dear." Cassandra smirked.

Ivan entered the building and headed to the back exit of the main room. He secured it with chains, then went and cut the alarm system and phone line. In the main room he could see some of the do-gooders sitting down.

He looked at the people who thought a night at the orphanage would earn them some good karma. Perhaps they thought the money they donated would help wash away the stink of sin on them. He smiled evilly, the things they didn't know, but would soon find out.

Ivan stepped up to the front of the room and cleared his throat.

"Excuse me everyone, I just want to remind you must turn in your cell phones before the recital. You'll get it back as soon as the recital's over." He held a tray and walked down the aisle, watching as people placed their cell phones on it, passing them down.

Humans were so stupid. A tap on his shoulder made him turn to see someone who must work there, due to the unhappy expression on their face.

"Excuse me sir, can I talk to you?"

Ivan smiled. "Of course."

Ivan followed the man to the back area. Before he had a chance to ask a question, or alert the others, he reached out and snapped the man's neck. He grabbed the body before it fell and placed it in a back chair out of the way. The corpse situated so it looked like it was leaning against the wall catching a nap.

Ivan was about to go out and get Cassandra when he saw the children entering. There were twenty-five of them. Cassandra would be pleased. Once outside he walked over to his love. He leaned in and kissed her as he removed the blindfold.

"Happy Solstice love, hope you like my gift."

Ivan grabbed her hand and led her inside. As soon as Casandra saw the children her fangs began to show. She turned to look at him and smiled hungrily.

"All of this for me?"

Ivan nodded his head. "All of them."

"The smell of innocence on the children, and the stink of sin on the adults. I'm intoxicated by it. When do we start?"

"In a few minutes, let everyone get seated. Then I'll lock the front entrance."

The two vampires took a seat in the back. Cassandra began to salivate. Ivan had done well. In just a few moments the massacre would start.

* * *

Derek got there just as they were closing the front doors. He entered the main room where all the kids and adults were. The two vampires were in the back. He had moments before he put his plan into motion. He needed the vampires to stay in the room, but didn't want people to die.

He watched as the male got up and began to walk towards him, chain in hand. Derek went off to the side, and sat. As the vampire went by Derek sighed in relief, then he heard a voice.

"Wait, let me in please."

"Of course, please come in."

Derek turned and saw Calvin. What the hell was he doing here? Hadn't he told him to stay put for the night. Derek reached out and grabbed Calvin. He looked over Calvin's shoulder and watched the vampire loop the chains around the doors and then place a lock on them.

"What are you doing here? I told you to stay home."

"Ow, you're hurting me." Someone a row ahead turned to look at Derek.

"Sorry, I didn't mean that. But you shouldn't be here, it's dangerous."

Calvin gave him a look of disbelief. "An orphan choir, how is that dangerous?"

"Calvin there are things you don't understand-"

At that moment the two vampires stood.

"Alright everyone, hope you had a nice dinner, because you're our dessert."

Derek watched as the male leaped the bench and grabbed a woman by the beck. He sunk his teeth in causing blood to spray everywhere. At the same moment the female grabbed a woman and pulled her head to the side so hard she almost ripped it clear off.

Chaos ensued, people ran to get out of doors that were now chained, kids were screaming and crying, and the people in charge of the orphanage seemed to have no idea what to do. Derek grabbed his bag and opened it. Reaching in, he pulled out a cross and handed it to Calvin.

"You take this, if those two come near you, wave it at them." Calvin stared at the vampires in disbelief.

"Calvin, do you understand? I'm going to clear the back exit, when I do you make a run for it." The boy slowly looked to Derek and nodded.

Derek hid Calvin in the corner near the front doors, then took the bolt cutters to the back exit. He cut the chain and got the attention of one of the employees.

"Get the kids out of here, come on move."

One of the adults noticed the open door and a stampede began. They were pushing kids out of the way, not caring who got crushed or hurt. Derek didn't have time to deal with it. Two very angry vampires were staring at him. The room had almost emptied, but they had time to kill at least four people.

"You, you're the one that's been following me."

"Yep, ridding the world of garbage like you is my job."

The vampire smiled. "Not for long."

The male vampire lunged at Derek, he grabbed a stake and a cross from his bag. When the vampire landed on him he held the cross to its face. Smoke began to rise and the vampire let out an enraged growl. Derek reached back to drive the stake in, but felt himself being lifted then flying through the air towards the wall.

When he hit he felt something crack, but didn't care at the moment. The vampire was bearing down on him fast, he had to move. Derek didn't even have time to stand before the vampire was there pulling him up and leaning in towards his neck.

With all his strength Derek kicked the vampire in the groin, not very effective, but enough to get his attention. Reaching into his pocket he grabbed a vial of holy water and jammed it in the mouth of the vampire. When it came into contact with the vampire it exploded violently. Derek felt warm fluid across his face, then he felt himself being tossed again, this time into the wooden doors chained shut. When he fell to the ground he saw Calvin huddled in the corner. He tried to motion with his eyes for the boy to run.

"Stupid human, you think that will stop me." The vampire spit out broken bits of glass.

Derek might not have dealt a serious blow, but it was something. He stood and faced the vampire. The female watched with interest, she had trapped about half a dozen adults in a corner.

She held one in front her by the neck. With a smile she twisted, and the sickening crack echoed throughout the room.

"This is for ruining my Solstice." She then began to suck on the neck of the body she held in her hands.

Derek had to save Calvin, try and save those people, and he had to kill two vampires. This plan seemed a lot better when he was sitting in his office. He had his gun, but it was too early to bring that out.

Derek went for his bag. The male vampire watched with interest, as if Derek was nothing more than a pet which amused him. He had seconds to find something useful. He put on the brass knuckles for no other reason than he might get lucky and land a punch. More vials of holy water were jammed into his pocket, a few stakes into his coat pocket, and then he felt it, a knife.

He pulled it out slowly and watched the male vampire as he circled him. Derek positioned himself so Calvin would not be visible in the background. Then he began to walk forward, directly towards the vampire.

A brief moment of shock crossed his face, then it went blank again.

"I like that, a man who comes to his death." The vampire smiled, his fangs in full view.

The screams of the adults left alive was background noise. Derek could only focus on the thing in front of him. As he got closer the vampire came at him. They hit one another and the noise sounded like thunder in the room. Derek had the air knocked out of him, and the vampire now had a knife deep in his chest.

The knife would not kill him, but it would stop him for a few seconds. In those seconds Derek was able to pull out a stake. The vampire backed away from him stumbling a bit. He looked down at the knife and laughed.

"This won't kill me you fool." Derek smiled.

"No it won't, but this sure as hell will." Derek jammed the stake as hard as he could into the chest of the vampire.

Shock clearly written across his face, the vampire looked down at the stake embedded in his heart. The female screamed and tossed the body she had been holding to the side. She was next to her male as he hit the ground.

"Ivan, no you can't die. Stay with me."

Ivan looked up and reached a smoking hand to her face. "Cassandra, I'm sorry I didn't top last year's Solstice." Then he slowly turned into a pile of smoking ash.

In the background Derek watched the other adults making their escape. He could sense Calvin was still there, too scared to move.

Cassandra let out a scream so shrill Derek had to cover his ears. She stood and shook the dust off of her.

"You'll die for this!" She lunged at Derek with the knife he had sunk into the chest of Ivan.

Derek felt the knife sink into his shoulder. The pain was excruciating, but he didn't make any noise. She twisted it around with a cruel smile on her face.

Then it stopped. Derek realized she was scanning the room. She knew someone else was with them. She looked at Derek and kicked out his leg, he heard the sickening sound of his tibia as it snapped.

"Come on out boy, I know you're here. I can smell you, all that fear, you're making me hungry."

"Don't listen to her, stay where you are kid." The pain was obvious in Derek's voice.

"Child, if you make me angry I'll kill this nice man."

"Dammit don't listen to her, stay where you are." Cassandra twisted the knife and Derek could not hold in the scream.

Calvin slowly stood. He held the cross in front of him. Cassandra laughed at him as she approached.

"That's a nice token, your daddy give that to you?"

A second later she stood in front of Calvin, the smoking cross in her hand. Calvin paled and looked to Derek for help.

"Leave him alone, he's just a kid. Or are you not strong enough to finish me off?"

Cassandra turned and looked at Derek. She grabbed Calvin by the collar and brought him over to where Derek had pulled himself into a sitting position.

"You think you can beat me hunter?"

"Yeah I do." Derek used one of the benches to stand, his broken leg useless, though he still towered over her by almost a foot.

Without thinking he swung his fist, the brass knuckles coated with holy water leaving a burn mark. Shock showed on Cassandra's face, and she automatically hit him back. Derek's head was rocked to the side and he spit out a molar when he regained his balance.

"You boy, what's your name?" Calvin looked to Derek.

Derek grabbed a handful of the holy water vials from his pocket and brought his hand up to her face. He smashed them so hard against her face they all shattered. She screamed as smoke rose from her melting skin. The left side of her face began to sag as the holy water destroyed parts of her eye, cheek, and nose.

Derek wanted to tell Calvin to run but he knew if he did the vampire would kill him instantly. Instead he had to time his next move perfectly.

"You'll pay for that." She sounded odd, the half of her face missing making speech difficult.

Derek knew whatever she did within the next few seconds would hurt. His mind was racing as he tried to figure out what to do. He had to save the boy. If he accomplished nothing else, Calvin at the least needed to live. He knew there was no bargaining with a vampire.

Cassandra reached for the knife in his shoulder and yanked it out. Derek almost threw up at the pain it caused. She held it up to her mouth and licked his blood off of it. Derek slowly reached behind him for his gun. He pulled it out and started to fire as soon as he brought it round to the front.

Cassandra now had at least six holes smoking in her torso. Derek realized he had not hit the heart. He still had a few shots, but Cassandra hit him causing him to fall back and stumble over the chairs.

"That was very naughty. Now the boy dies." Cassandra placed her hands on Calvin's shoulders and lifted him.

"No he doesn't."

Derek lifted the gun and fired aiming for whatever these things called a heart. He knew he scored a direct hit when Cassandra jerked and let go of Calvin.

"Run, get out of here now."

"What about you?"

"Calvin, get out of here now!" Derek sighed in relief when he saw Calvin relent and run out the back exit. At least the boy would make it.

Cassandra was still standing, her body shaking violently. Then she exploded into bits and pieces of bloody goop. She wasn't as old as the other one, she was still a bit fresh. The fresh ones took longer to die, and when they did they left a disgusting mess behind.

"Excuse me is anyone in here, a little boy outside said his dad is in here." Derek smiled at the thought.

"Yeah over here."

A moment later a paramedic was talking into a walkie-talkie about him and needing some help. He knew the shoulder and leg looked worse than they were, but he had to admit they hurt like a son of a bitch.

Derek was loaded onto a stretcher then loaded into an ambulance. Calvin insisted on going with him, because it was his dad. Derek smiled as he lost consciousness.

* * *

Derek woke up to the sound of his bedroom door opening. He had gotten home from the hospital a few days ago. Calvin had the house decked out for Christmas even though it was a few days late. They ate junk food and watched movies since Derek had a broken leg and some serious damage to his shoulder.

Calvin loved the gadgets Derek had gotten him, but the best was when he presented the papers to become Calvin's legal guardian.

Of course he would need to be more careful now when he worked, but he could handle it. Looking into the face of Calvin, he knew the kid could handle it to.

"Hey Derek are you making pancakes today?"

"I will, just give me a minute to get up."

"You know there's no way you're gonna be able to top this Christmas right?"

Derek just smiled as he forced himself out of bed to make pancakes. How life can change in so short a time. Perhaps some things were just meant to be.

Not Many Vampires

OR, HOW WINTER STOPPED A TRANSDIMENSIONAL CREATURE FROM DEVOURING THE WORLD/RUINING CHRISTMAS WITHOUT BREAKING A NAIL

STORY: PATRICK SHAND   ART: RACHEL DUKES

Story Art Cover
By Rachel Dukes
www.poseurink.com

Dedication

This story is for my mom, who has been reading about these characters for years and years.

It's also for Chris, who has been telling me I should stop messing around and get a story set in this universe published. Oh yeah, shameless plug: Winter is part of a larger story called THE CONTINUITY, coming to your local bookstores hopefully before I die.

It's also for Roger Dupre, who told me from the beginning that Winter was my most interesting character.

Lastly, it's for Erica. But then, everything I write is for this wonderful girl, so that's no surprise.

Author Bio

PATRICK SHAND would like to wish you a merry Christmas... as long as you promise not to play that Alvin and the Chipmunks song. In addition to writing stories about snarky and morally ambiguous vampires in charity anthologies, Patrick has written for Joss Whedon's ANGEL comic book... which, okay, yes, is also about snarky and morally ambiguous vampires. He has also written for Spike TV & Zenescope Entertainment's 1000 WAYS TO DIE comic and various anthologies published by Pill Hill Press, Rainstorm Press, and more. You can read about Patrick (and his character Winter, the snarky and morally... you get the point) at patrick-shand.blogspot.com.

Not Many Vampires

or, How Winter Stopped a Transdimensional Creature from Devouring the World/Ruining Christmas Without Breaking a Nail
By Patrick Shand

Not many vampires can say that they spent Christmas Eve draining Santa Clause, can they?

Well, my name is Winter... and I'm not many vampires. Merry Christmas.

Granted, the victim in question was a mall Santa that I found walking to his car in the deserted parking lot behind the Macy's, but *still*, right? Hell of a way to celebrate the holidays.

It went a little something like this.

I hit the mall a bit after sunset. I usually won't go out shopping on a holiday, but sometimes an undead girl gets in the mood to buy some new shoes. What can I say? I'm a giver... to myself.

Anyway, after hours of waiting in line with humans who stank of sweat (not at all appetizing) I finally bought my *Merry Christmas to me* gift... which was the sexiest pair of boots I'd ever seen. Satisfied with my selection, I walked out of the store and passed a line of munchkins and bored mothers waiting to sit on Santa's lap. I thought how *delicious* it would be if I queued up with them, slid onto that jolly red lap, and gave good old Rosy Cheeks a long kiss on his neck. I could practically hear the first scream in my head, could almost see the mothers and children running as I pulled away from his gushing neck and screamed, "A merry Christmas to all, and to all a good night!" That would be *killer*.

But let's get real – I wanted to get back to my apartment and try on the boots. Priorities, you know? So I took the subway back to my place, which is pretty much a bare, almost empty room. While I prefer luxury, it's functional for what I need. A pretty face like mine can't stay in one town for very long or folks start recognizing me, which isn't really good for the whole *eating people* lifestyle. Anyway, I tried on the boots, put on a dress that I'd taken off my Thursday girl (that's how I refer to my victims—by the day of the week), and *look. At. Me.*

I'm not vain, but... hah, fuck it, of *course* I am. You would be too, in boots like these.

But then? I realized I didn't have much of a plan. I hit the clubs the night before, but I didn't feel like draining someone with a blood alcohol content of .37 two nights in a row. I went back to my Santa fantasy, and before I realized that I'd formulated a game plan, I was out the door. I mean, "go to mall, kill Santa, feel badass in new boots" isn't *much* of a game plan, but I like to take it easy for the holidays.

So, that's how I ended up gum-deep in Santa's jugular, sucking the *ho-ho-ho*s out of his throat. He was a struggler, and I liked that. As long as he didn't get blood on my boots, everything was copasetic. Santa flailed his arms about, which was entertaining at first, but I suddenly felt a sharp pain in the middle of my forehead.

"Ow!" I said. My mouth was a bit stifled by Santa's bloody neck, so it came out more like "Oughrl."

Wondering how the hell this fool hurt me, I dug my teeth even deeper into his throat so that my upper lip went under his skin. He moaned in pain as I smiled in his ruined flesh. And then—

"OWWWWW!" I cried. I fell back from Santa, sprawling on the pavement, clutching my forehead. I felt like I'd been shot through the skull by a bullet dipped in holy water. I watched Santa run away, leaving a train of blood as he fled. He'd probably drop dead a few blocks from there, but the way I felt, it looked as if he'd live longer than me. My vision started to blur, my face felt as if it were melting off, and... *fuck* – the last thing I saw before I everything went black was that I'd fallen in a puddle, covering my new boots in mud.

* * *

Not many vampires can say that they spent Christmas Eve with a mummy, a *Creature from the Black Lagoon* look-alike, a monster that looked like a wad of lo mein, a human, and a foul mouthed Will-o'-the-Wisp, can they?

Well, my name is Winter... and I'm not many vampires.

When I came to, I wasn't in a parking lot with Santa-blood caked onto my face. I was in what looked like a video game arcade except for the five monsters that stared down at me like I was a science fair project.

"She wakes!" The mummy cried, waving a bandaged hand to someone across the room. I couldn't see who (or what).

"Where am I?" I asked. I tried to leap to my feet, but found that my legs were weak and my head felt fuzzy. Even though the searing pain was gone, I didn't have much energy left. I felt like I'd been beaten up by an army. Since I couldn't get *up* to look at my kidnappers, I curled my lips back, hissed at them, and sat Indian style. I know, not the most intimidating position, but it was all I could manage.

I looked at each of them, already searching for weak points. Mummy boy was obviously a walking corpse covered in gauze, so a few well-placed blows might leave him limbless. Second up was a green, bony creature with the wide mouth of a fish, a neck slashed with hard gills, and feet that looked like moss covered pancakes. And—I guess there isn't a way to avoid this next bit sounding ridiculous—he wore a baby blue robe. Didn't think he'd give me much trouble. The same could be applied to the... *thing* to his right, a googly eyed creature made up of tentacles and tendrils and, debatably, pasta. Him, I could just boil in a pot and call it a day. A glowing orb of light floated over his shoulder. *This* one I knew.

"Will-o'-the-Wisp?" I said, finally gathering the strength to push myself up to my feet. "Who brings a Will-o'-the-Wisp to a monster fight?"

The Will-o'-the-Wisp got in my face and began to flash angrily, almost blinding me.

"*Shut up, vampire bitch!*" It cried in a voice that sounded like a robot on helium. "*Don't judge! Don't fucking judge me!*"

"Did you just call me a bitch, you little lightning bug?"

"*Die, unholy whore!*"

"Whoa, calm down Will-o'!" The mummy said, stepping between me and the flashing Wisp. Taking in a deep, rattle of a breath, the mummy held out a bandaged hand and smiled with mouth full of rotted teeth. "I'm Abubakar."

"I'm Wade," the fishman gurgled.

"Hey, I'm Timmy, nice to meet you," the pasta monster said, scratching his eyeball with a noodly appendage.

A human—a damn *pretty* hunk of a human that I wouldn't

have minded taking my sweet time draining—ran over. He saw Abubakar holding out a hand to me and then waved.

"Glad to see you're awake," he said. "I'm Reginald."

Completely baffled, I looked at Abubakar, who was still pitifully holding his hand there. No way I was going to introduce myself. First of all, I felt weird about introducing myself as Winter during the Christmas holidays; opens the floor up for way too many corny jokes at my expense. Second, who the hell *were* these guys anyway? I looked down at Abubakar's hand, rolled my eyes, and said, "Listen, sweetie, I wouldn't touch that thing through three gloves. May I just ask why the *hell* did you Universal Monsters rejects kidnap me?"

"Kidnap?" Abubakar cried, obviously offended. "*Us*? KIDNAP!? We're the SHM!"

"Oh, the SHM, great, good for you," I said. "What the hell is the SHM? It sounds like a men's magazine."

"The Society of Heroic Monsters!" they all said together. It was the lamest thing I have ever seen.

"You're shitting me," I said.

"Shit you not, dudette," Wade said. "Feel a little pain between the eyes before, did you? I hear that. I damn near busted a gill the first time that happened to me."

"The first time *what* happened, fish boy?" I said. "I'm going to start kicking asses and laughing at silly names if I don't stop getting more questions than answers. What the hell is this, *Lost*?"

Abubakar sighed. "We're the Society of—"

"Yes, you're the Society of Super Sissy Monsters, got it. Tell me what I'm doing here and why I shouldn't go all Buffy on your defanged asses."

Abubakar went to open his mouth again, but Reginald the increasingly tasty-looking human cleared his throat and stepped forward. "I've got this, Abu." The mummy nodded and began fiddling with one of his bandages, looking annoyed.

"Allow me to explain," Reginald said. "I don't know how long you've been hunting here... which, let me add, the SHM does *not* approve of, but that's neither here nor there... but what you experienced is not the first time this has happened to a supernatural creature... forgive me, supernatural *woman*... in this area."

74

Whew, did I ever want to suck his throat.

Reginald continued, saying, "I'm afraid that the reason the SHM has taken up residence in this area is because the local park has a very, very weak spot in the fabric of reality. There was a bit of an... incident involving our friend Will-o' earlier this year—"

The Wisp let out an annoyed sound that sounded like feedback on a radio. *"Oh, you just had to go and bring that up! You're a real son of a bitch, Reginald, do you know that? I told you a million goddamn times, I was just saying 'hello' to that fairy, we were* not *the cause of any rift, and--"*

"Enough, Willow," Abubakar said.

"Piss on you, Reginald! Piss on you!"

"Fine, yes, piss on me," Reginald said, laughing dismissively. When Will-o' buzzed off, he turned back to me and said, "Some Dimensioners... forgive me, humans who think it's *fun* to dabble in opening portals to other dimensions... have taken advantage of this local hotspot."

"Thanks for the exposition, Narrator, but what has that got to do with me waking up in a room with *I'm Not Scary* Anonymous?" I said.

"The SHM," Abubakar corrected under his breath.

"There is a certain creature that the Dimensioners have been attempting to unleash on our world. To what end, we don't know. But the creature cannot travel across dimensions in its true form. It must possess someone from our plane of existence in order to step into our world. A human body cannot stand the power of the beast, though... so the Dimensioners have been attempting to kidnap supernatural creatures. They blow a... special whistle, creating a sound that is unbearably painful to supernatural beings. I heard rumblings that they were going to attempt to rip open reality again tonight, so Abukabar and I went on patrol... and found you, luckily before they did."

Ah. A whistle. Like I'm a damn dog. Great. I needed to get me a set of earplugs.

"So I guess that's why a midnight snack like you works with these guys?" I said. "You're the only one that wouldn't be affected."

"When I was younger, I dabbled in dimensional rifts," he

said. "I know how dangerous the practice can be. I joined the SHM in order to prevent creatures like whatever they're trying to call from crossing over into our world."

"Fun," I said, deciding I'd had enough of my Supernatural History 101 for one day. As much as I wanted to eat and maybe also lick Reginald, I was about ready to call it a night. But one thing was bothering me.

I was barefoot.

"I'm gonna go," I said. "But first, why the hell are my boots not on my feet? And don't *tell* me the mummy touched them, because... ew."

"I've never!" Abubakar cried and stormed away, pieces of gauze flapping behind him.

"Oh, yeah, no shoes allowed on the carpet. Avoids stains. Don't worry, I'll get the boots," Wade said, walking across the room, his feet slapping on the floor with wet smacks.

"Reginald, you didn't tell her the best part!" Timmy the tentacled thing said. "Tell her about the prophecy!"

From opposite sides of the room, Abubakar and Reginald simultaneously shot Timmy what had to be the dirtiest looks I'd ever seen. And trust me, I've received some *glares* in my life.

Timmy shrank back, his eyes retreating into the slimy squiggles of his head. "What?"

Sighing, Reginald looked at me, appearing to be almost embarrassed. "There's a bit more," he said.

"Don't care," I said.

"There's a prophecy."

"Don't care."

"You're going to save the day, vampire. And that day just happens to be Christmas, if a prophecy alone weren't silly enough."

"Don't... wait, are you *freakin' serious*?" I said. "You have a prophecy that says that I'm going to *save Christmas*? Sarcastic emphasis very, very much intended."

Wade came jogging back up, the boots in his hands. "Here you go. Ugh, jeez, how did these get so dirty? Looks like you stepped in mud."

Happy fucking Holidays.

* * *

Not many vampires can say that they spent Christmas Eve unintentionally saving the world from transdimensional monsters, can they?

Well, my name is Winter... and I'm not many vampires.

A prophecy. An actual prophecy. A prophecy that said, and I directly quote, "On the Eve, a heroic vampire will stop the Mover of Worlds from devouring the Earth with a human by her side." I mean... *really*? Who writes these things anyway?

Naturally, when I first heard the prophecy, I laughed my ass off, grabbed my boots, and left the arcade. I mean, what kind of League of Entirely *Not* Extraordinary Gentlemen houses up in an arcade anyway? What's with that?

But when I was half a block away, I stopped. Started thinking. What if one of those fools from the SHM got caught by these Dimensioner guys... hell, they'd be *easy* bait. Any schlup off the street could just throw Wade or Abubakar or that annoying little firefly into the rift and whatever beastie trying to step through will have a sudden all-access pass to our dimension which, according to the prophecy, will then get *devoured*. Now, don't get me wrong. I'm no "heroic vampire." The mere existence of those movies with the poofy haired pseudo-vamps drooling over that retarded girl makes me want to kill a baby with an ice pick. I fully subscribe to the whole evil bloodlust thing. But when it comes to a monster trying to *eat* my dimension... thing is, I'm part of this dimension.

So that doesn't work for me.

I turned around, ready to march back to the SHM arcade, and saw Reginald walking up the block toward me with a satchel hanging from his shoulder.

"Going somewhere?" he asked, smirking.

"Get cute and you die," I said. "I did some thinking."

"No need to explain," he said.

"You're one to talk, Mr. I Speak In Block Quotes."

"Clever. Shall we?"

"Fulfill the lamest prophecy I've ever heard in my life?" I said. "Yeah, let's go. Fighting monsters alongside of a human. Never would've guessed I'd spend Christmas Eve like this?"

"How *did* you picture spending it?" Reginald asked. If I didn't know better, I'd say he was attempting to flirt with me from the way he kept smirking that strange little smirk. Well...

come to think, I don't know better. Of damn course he was flirting with me. Mud on my boots or not, I'm the center of attention even when a big ol' baddie is about to make a transdimensional trip.

"Buying boots, killing Santa," I said. "You know. The ushe."

We were kind of quiet the rest of the way there. I guess talking about the attempted murder of childhood icons is a bit of a conversation killer. Oh well. We all have our weaknesses.

We got to the empty park and set up shop right under the weak spot in the fabric of reality. While I twiddled my thumbs, absolutely clueless, Reginald took some candles, a jar of blood (smelled like virgin), and a knife. With a quick strike of a match, he lit the candles and untwisted the jar of blood.

"Mind if I give it a taste test?" I asked. "Just, you know, to make sure it's kosher?"

"After," he said, lowering the knife into the jar. It came out red and dripping. I don't know what it was about seeing him with that bloody knife, but I just wanted to rip his clothes off and ride him until sunrise. While killing him, obviously.

"What's the blood for anyway?" I asked.

Reginald took a step forward, his eyes darting around as if he were looking for something in the middle of the air. His eyes settled on a spot that looked absolutely no different than the rest. He smiled.

"How are you feeling?" he asked. "Up for a brawl?"

"I'm only here because that damn prophecy says we win," I said. "I honestly still feel like I got staked. That whistle thing really knocked it out of me."

"Good, good," Reginald said, holding the bloody knife up to the spot. He stabbed the air and tore the knife down, leaving a glowing golden slash in its wake. "To answer your question, the blood is used as a tool to tear reality and open a door to another dimension."

I started at Reginald, his handsome face illuminated from the glow of the dimensional rift. Chuckling, realization setting in, I said, "Don't tell me you wrote that prophecy."

"Sure did," he said. "Wrote it as soon as I saw you. Distracted Abubakar for a moment, blew my whistle, you passed out, and then I took you back to the headquarters—"

"Arcade," I corrected.

"—*arcade* and rambled on and on about this prophecy. There have been no Dimensioners other than me, vampire. I joined the SHM, bragging about my knowledge of dimensions and how I can help them take down creatures worse than they could even imagine. But all the while, I've been testing each of them, seeing if any of them are strong enough to be the host... None were powerful enough. And then, vampire, I found you. The perfect host, the perfectly *strong*, perfectly *evil* creature to—"

"Why even take me back to the SHM? Why not take me here while I was knocked out?"

"If I were a gentleman, I'd tell you that it was because Abubakar returned and saw me with you... or that the ritual must be performed at a certain hour... and both of those are true. But really? I needed you weakened but conscious, because I sure as hell couldn't carry you."

Ouch.

"I'm going to savor this kill," I said, baring my fangs.

The gash in reality suddenly tripled in size, and the blinding glow was making my eyes water. I could see tentacles slapping around on the inside, teeth gnashing, claws swiping. It was happening.

"You cannot stop the arrival, vampire, for the time of man has—"

"Okay, sorry to interrupt again," I said, "but you seem to be under the impression that I give a tiny little shit about your plan. I don't. It's boring. You're boring. The SHM is lame and I don't care that you betrayed those guys. Hell, I planned on killing you as soon as we got rid of this thing."

"Fine," Reginald said. "I guess I'll just have to *make* you care."

He dove towards me faster than I expected. He swung the knife at me, narrowly missing my neck. I avoided the next two times he slashed at me, but I was still woozy from the whistle, and the giant glowing creature made of pure unharnessed energy that was sliding out of the hole was pretty disconcerting. The thing wanted to possess me and then eat the damn world, and here I was fending off an over-sharer with a hard-on for dramatic flair.

I don't know how he did it, but Reginald managed to sweep

my feet out from under me. He stepped on my chest, pinning me to the ground. The monster's energy spilled toward us, pulsating, glowing, ready to consume me.

"Still weakened," Reggie said, that annoying little smirk creeping on his face. He reached into his pocket and pulled out a wooden whistle that had strange symbols carved into it. "Get ready to be taken over by—"

"Blah blah blah! God! Bad news, Reggie boy," I said. With all of my remaining strength, I brought my leg up, kicking him in between the legs with the toe of my brand new boots. The whistle fell from his hands and he slammed into the ground, clutching himself. I stood up, brushing my dress off. "My *not so good* is still better than your one hundred percent."

I reached down and picked him up by the throat, feeling a hell of a lot more like myself now that I was in control of the situation. Bringing him close to me, I dug my fangs into his neck and took a quick drink. Eh. He tasted okay. You build something up so much, the results are usually disappointing.

And plus, the glowing mass of demonic energy spilling out of the hole in reality seemed to suggest that there were more immediate concerns than draining Reginald.

Oh.

I looked from Reginald to the energy. From the energy to Reginald. I grinned.

"Hey," I said. "So if this thing needs a supernaturally strong host to harness its power... I wonder what would happen if—"

And then I threw him at it. He hit the energy and began to shake violently. Tendrils of glowing *power* flowed up his nostrils, into his mouth, into his chest. I took a step back, shielding my eyes. As he disappeared into the glow, I could swear that I heard him squeak out, "don't you want to hear my motivation?"

I considered shouting out a reminder that I didn't care, but something told me he couldn't hear me.

With a flash, the glow dissipated and all that was left was a squirming, bloated Reginald in the middle of the park. To my intense surprise, he stood up, shook himself off, and stared at me with the most horrifying green eyes I'd ever seen. For the first time that night—hell, for the first time *ever* – I was scared.

Reginald took a step toward me and, with a wet *splortch*,

hundreds of tentacles popped out of his back. His hands began to reform into claws on top of claws, his bones snapping and growing with wet pops and hollow crunches. "I feel it," he said, speaking with a thousand different voices at once. The sound brought me to my knees, and I realized that he would probably be able to kill me with a word. His voice made it feel as if my marrow were on fire. "I feel the power."

His head began to swell.

His chest started to bubble as if he were boiling.

His mouth burst open with teeth growing on top of teeth, on top of teeth.

"The... power," he said with all of his terrible voices.

And then, his head exploded, showering everything in sight (including my poor, beautiful, new boots) with putrid, steaming muck. What was left of Reginald slithered around aimlessly until it melted into a dark stain on the ground.

I wiped the remains off of my face, stood up, and let out of a loud laugh. "I guess *that's* what happens when you do that."

* * *

I went back to the arcade. Don't ask me why. I guess I maybe wanted to gloat a bit about the prophecy.

I gathered Abubakar, Wade, Timmy, and Will-o' around. I cleared my throat and then said, "Hand in hand, Reginald and I defeated the monster from across the way *together*, as the prophecy said. He fought valiantly and died a hero. He took the monster down, forever closing the hole, repairing damage to reality... I will remember his last words for the rest of my life. He said... he said, 'Tell the SHM that...' Okay, wow, I'm sorry, this is just too funny. I'm totally messing with you guys. He betrayed you. He opened the hole and tried to use me as the host so I exploded him. End of story. Tell your friends."

The SHM stared at me like a bunch of hurt puppies, and that, my friends, is the best Christmas gift I could have ever asked for. I laughed so hard that it hurt my throat and, by the time I finished making fun of them, I realized that I'd royally messed up by returning to the arcade. The big funky clock on the scoreboard above the mini bowling alley said that it was nearly sunrise. The ordeal with Reginald had taken the entire night, and now I wasted my last precious hour of night making fun of these idiots for their friend's betrayal.

Damn. Freaking karma.

Abubakar came over to me, seeing that I'd stopped laughing hysterically. "I am deeply saddened by this news," he said. "Reginald, a traitor..."

"I'm deeply saddened that it's almost daylight," I said. "I'm stuck in an arcade with *you* guys. I think I might stake myself."

Abubakar shook his head, frowning deeply. "I fear that I may regret this, seeing as you are a murderer and *worse...* a mocker of the great and noble SHM... but Wade has asked me to extend an invite to you. We are having Christmas dinner here today, and—"

"Seriously?" I interrupted.

He nodded, his bandages shifting down over his head, revealing a spot of rotten scalp. He moved the gauze back, clearly embarrassed.

I looked at Wade, who was playing a dance game by himself, his floppy feet slapping around like fish on a deck. I looked at Timmy and that potty mouthed Will-o'-the-Wisp cheering Wade on. For a brief moment, I pictured myself drinking a cup of blood next to them, telling them the full story of what happened with Reginald. Might be not entirely terrible to have someone to tell stories to on Christmas.

Ah. But...

"You're totally going to try to convince me to become the lamest vampire in the world and join your pansy ass club, aren't you?" I asked.

"Well..." Abubakar said.

"You are! And you're also going to warn me against killing!" I cried.

"Killing is wrong!"

"You're a monster, you idiot! It's the only thing you're good for! Well, *you'd* be amazing at teepeeing a house, I must say," I said, pulling on one of his bandanges.

"*Don't touch his fucking wrappings, vampire bitch!*" Will-o' screeched, flying over to me. "*He's sensitive about that!*"

"Get laid, firefly."

"*You dare!? Piss on you, vampire! Piss on you!*"

So that whole dinner scenario got ruined quickly. I did the good villain thing (gave them all the finger and promised to come back and kill them at a later date) and ran out the door. Gotta love boots that not only make you look hot but also don't get in the way of running. I'd have to see if I could get the mud and transdimensional innards out with some good ol' soap and water.

I managed to get underground before sunrise. Ugh. Sleeping in the subway. It would be a gross way to spend Christmas, but I wasn't sure if I could deal with more excitement anyway. I mean, I spent the holiday killing Santa, ruining my beautiful new boots, making fun of the most ridiculous collection of creatures under the sun, finding out a whole bunch of useless information about dimensions, defeating a creature from who *knows* where, and—craziest of all—getting invited to share Christmas dinner with a room full of do-gooders. Man, I'd have to kill a few priests to get the sickly sweet taste of that last one out.

But really, how many vampires could say *that's* how they spent their holiday?

Well, in case you hadn't heard, my name is Winter... and I'm not many vampires.

Story Art Cover
By David Naughton-Shires
http://www.TheImageDesigns.com

Dedication
To my older brother Scott, for not only taking me, but paying my way to so many of those late, great, cheesy horror films of the 80's.

Author Bio
Matt Kurtz writes twisted tales for fun in his spare time. His fiction can be found in anthologies from Pill Hill Press, Evil Jester Press, Blood Bound Books, Comet Press, and Necrotic Tissue Magazine.

Ol' Creepy In A Red Suit
Matt Kurtz

Little Joey was all alone in the dark house when he heard the footsteps on the roof. He dropped his horror comic book on top of the desk and stared at the ceiling. Frozen, he sat waiting for another noise to confirm it wasn't his overactive imagination after reading such ghastly tales on the printed page.

Thump. *Thump.*

Joey started from the sound, now louder and directly above his head. He quickly fumbled with the tabletop lamp and clicked it off. Sliding out of his chair, he hid in the murky area under the desk. The red bulb Christmas lights stapled to the overhang just outside his window flashed in a one second tempo, making the place look as if it was lit by a neon sign at some flea bag motel, or worse, the red-light district in Amsterdam.

After a few moments of silence, Joey popped his head out from under the desk and gazed upwards. He hoped that he killed the lamp in time before whoever was up there saw its golden light and discovered that he was home alone; especially if it was that lunatic responsible for butchering people while they slept and terrorizing the community for the past two weeks. The authorities were baffled by the drastic differences in a couple of the recent murders. Some of the bodies were found intact but completely drained of blood, the premises spotless, while others were hacked into tiny pieces and the crime scene an utter bloodbath. Was the butcher being fickle with his modus operandi? Trying new things out? Or, God forbid, could it be possible that there were *two* serial killers stalking the area? The only lead the police had was the statement of a seven-year old that witnessed a big fat man dressed as Santa Clause on his neighbor's roof the night one of the families was slaughtered. Although a child seeing Santa during Christmastime wasn't the most promising lead, it carried more weight than the proposed alternative put forth by the scared citizens at an emergency town meeting: satanic hippy drifters sacrificing for the Devil himself. When in doubt, blame Beelzebub!

Now to Joey, the thought of some maniac sneaking down chimneys dressed as Ol' Saint Nick, butchering people in their sleep, really gave him the willies. He already had in inherent fear of the fatty in a red suit, finding it extremely creepy that people not only expected, but *wanted* the rotund fellow to slip into their homes while they slept. His skin really crawled over the tales of kids leaving out Oreos and milk for the man, only to find the half-devoured cookies plated next to an empty glass the next morning.

Clump...*thump*—both from above!

Joey flinched and pulled back under the desk like a turtle retreating in its shell. Wide-eyed with dread, his bulging orbs seemed to glow in the dark.

Someone was definitely up there, all right.

It had to be *him*. The psycho Killer Santa.

Joey sucked in a breath and puffed up, making his scrawny chest bigger. It was time to step up and defend the homestead. Was he really going to allow some madman to drop down the chimney and trespass in his sanctuary?

The clunking of heavy steps moved across the ceiling...toward the chimney.

Joey sprung into action, grabbing a handful of horror comics from the floor and quickly flipping through them.

"Read it...read it...read it...read it..." He stopped on one in particular, "*Gotta* read it," and tossed the comic on the bed. Joey quickly resumed his separation of what comics he *had* read and those he *needed* to read. Once there were enough to build a decent fire with, he took the "have reads" and a pack of matches from the desk drawer and ran out of the room.

He stopped at the top of the landing and stared down into the shadowy abyss that swallowed the bottom half of the stairs. A second later, the red string of lights flashed outside the windows, sending the entire house into the same color of a scorching stovetop coil. Then the first floor was gone again, just a wall of black. Then it lit red. This continued in a steady rhythm, making Joey feel a little disoriented and a lot scared.

He stood frozen, listening. Had he taken too long with all his comic sorting? Was the psychopath already inside, down there...waiting for him? A chill snaked up his spine at the very thought.

Another thump came from the ceiling above. Joey flinched at the sound and instinctively ducked. Although the fat guy was still outside, he was definitely on the move again, heading in the chimney's direction.

Joey ran down the stairs, his bare feet drumming the thick carpeted steps, and swung around the corner into the living room.

A dark rain of ash and soot fell behind the cast iron fireplace screen and onto the empty steel grate. Joey slid up to the hearth and tossed aside the heavy screen.

Scraping noises and grunts echoed down the flue, causing the golden peach fuzz on Joey's neck to prickle. He had to work fast before it was too late. Balling the comics into a wad, he tossed them onto the grate and pulled out the matchbook.

Striking one on the phosphorous strip, the match sparked but only smoked, failing to ignite. Joey threw it down and tried another. The noises in the flue were getting louder. He could faintly make out the incoherent mumbles and grumbles of the fat man working his way down. Getting closer.

Joey struck another match with trembling hands and missed the strip all together. His next attempt was successful and the match lit, its flame illuminated his face in a warm yellow glow, erasing all trace of the crimson tint from the outside lights.

Joey held the match to the comics and smiled as they began to burn. Taking a few steps back, he watched as the flames grew, filling the entire hearth.

Retching hacks and coughs sounded from the flue as the dark plumes of smoke rose.

Joey's grin spread, nearly splitting his face in two. "Burn, ya fat bastard. Burn!"

Then the fire started to recede; its orange glow lessened. Joey's smile faded in unison with the dying flames as the comics quickly turned from inferno to smoldering ash.

What was he thinking? In order to sustain the fire, he needed kindling. Wood.

A hack of phlegm came down the flue. Then more soot fell. The man was on the move again.

This guy just isn't givin' up, Joey thought, then took a deep breath. *But neither am I.*

He ran to the middle of the living room and looked around for something to burn. Then it hit him. There was a huge pile of magazines beside the upstairs toilet in the master bathroom. He could retrieve the periodicals and smash one of the dining room chairs to use as kindling. That should get a decent fire going.

Joey ducked out of the room and flew up the stairs.

A few minutes later, he returned with his arms full and skidded to a stop.

"Oh, no..."

The stack of magazines fell to the ground and landed on the carpet...beside the large sooty footprints coming out of the fire-place. Standing frozen, only his eyes followed the prints across the room as each step slightly faded with less of an ashy im-print. The tracks disappeared around the corner and into the kitchen.

A jingle of bells sounded over Joey's shoulder.

He tensed then spun around.

Nothing.

The wood floor creaked somewhere in the dining room. Around the corner by the staircase. Near the second entrance to the kitchen.

During the red blinking lights, Joey saw the large shadow elongating from around the corner and across the dining room floor.

No, not elongating. Moving closer.

Joey sprung forward, praying he could still make it up the stairs in time to barricade himself behind a locked bedroom door. Making it the base of the stairs, he planted his foot on the first step when a white gloved hand lashed out from around the corner and clamped over his shoulder, stopping him dead in his tracks.

Bound by dread, Joey refused to turn around. The gloved hand stretching out of the red sleeve with a white furry cuff was enough to tell him that his worst nightmare was coming true.

"And where do ya think you're going, little fella?" A deep voiced asked, its hot breath so close that Joey felt it blow across his nape, raising gooseflesh the size of Ping-Pong balls.

Joey screamed. He ducked, dropping to all fours, and kicked back with all his might. When his foot made contact with the man, he heard a guttural groan then a few clunky steps across the entryway's wooden floor.

Free from the psychotic fatty's grasp, Joey scrambled up the steps and shrieked in horror.

"Get back here, ya little bastard!" The man yelled from the bottom of the stairs. "Ho-ho-ho, do I got a little something for ya!"

Still hunched over, Joey clawed at the steps to aid in his speedy ascent. Reaching the landing, he whipped around the corner and sprinted to the bedroom. With his sanctuary in sight, Joey glanced over his shoulder and saw the enormous shadow moving up the stairs.

When he looked back a second time, the super-sized killer was standing atop the landing, facing Joey. He was in full Father Christmas apparel, from his black boots to ivory beard to the white fuzzy ball adorning his red stocking cap. The only thing that seemed a little unseasonal during such a cheerful holiday was the enormous Bowie knife he held in his hand, clumps of hair and dried blood staining its polished blade.

Joey screamed and barreled into the bedroom. Whirling around to shut the door, the outside lights flashed, illuminating the killer Santa Clause, now bug-eyed and halfway down the hallway, charging at Joey.

Joey shrieked again and slammed his door. Just as he flipped the lock on its handle, his attacker plowed into it, causing the door to bend inward then snap back against its frame.

Spinning around, Joey looked at the bedroom window and saw it was frozen shut. The door was slammed upon again with such force it caused the wood to crack.

"Little pig, little pig, let me in!" came from the other side.

Joey eyed his potential hiding places, the closed closet or under the bed. His breathing grew shallow from the extreme adrenaline rush. His chest tightened. Although he couldn't believe this was happening, he was more afraid of what might happen next.

There was a loud crack then part of the molding on the doorframe exploded into splinters of wood. The bedroom door flew open, lopsided and barely attached to its hinges. The Killer Santa entered and saw the boy's pajama clad leg disappear under the bed skirt. The lunatic carefully closed the damaged door behind him and tipped over the large dresser in front of it, blocking the only way out of the room.

"C'mon out, boy. Ain't no one gonna help ya." The man made his way toward the bed shoved against the wall, his heavy weight causing the floor to creak.

Joey slid as far back as possible until his back was flush with the wall. He was trapped like an animal. As scared as he was, there was only one thing left to do.

"Don't ya wanna come out to get your present?" The killer asked, slowly waving the large knife through the air. "Don't matter if ya been naughty or nice. You *all* get what's comin' to ya in the end." The man smiled behind his false, shaggy beard that looked more like a wet poodle glued to his cheeks. He paused and took a step back.

"Hmmmm....ya know, maybe I should check the closet." Was he trying to taunt Joey? Drive him to the brink of madness by his own dread? (The man was a psychopath after all.)

With his eyes glued to the bed, in case Joey tried to make a run for it, Santa sidestepped his way over to the closet. Placing his gloved hand on the knob, he twisted and ripped open the door.

"Hmmmmm....." he said, his eyes still on the bed, "nothing in here but—"

He casually turned and glanced into the closet. Having to do a double take at the sight within, his mouth went agape. "What the..." was all he could muster as he fumbled for the light inside.

When the dark closet lit up, the current residents of the house, a family of four, were slumped in a pile of entwined limbs on the floor like a mound of dirty laundry. Their flesh was marble-like. Their blood drained from their bodies through the two tiny and bruised puncture wounds in their necks. While the mother and father faced one another in a death's embrace, the two young boys stared up with lifeless eyes at the man dressed as Kris Kringle.

Santa shook his head then shrugged and snickered. He made his way back to the bed. "Holy shit, boy, " he said, thumbing over his shoulder to the bloodless corpses in the closet, "What the hell did that?"

He bent down on all fours, groaning as his knees popped loudly. The man lifted the bed skirt and squinted into the

92

darkness beyond.

Two glowing orbs stared back at him.

"I did," Joey answered from the blackness, his raspy voice immediately turning into a snarl.

A small, pale, taloned hand shot out from under the bed and grabbed the man by the neck. Before he could scream, fingernails tore into flesh then the hand ripped back, disappearing under the skirt again.

The man lifted his head, blood and breath gurgling out of the gaping hole in his throat. Crouched on all fours, his rubbery limbs gave out, and he dropped flat on the floor.

The taloned hand shot out again, its index and middle fingers hooking deep into the man's eye sockets like a bowling bowl, puncturing his eyeballs with a wet popping sound. The hand viciously yanked the man under the bed by his bloody sockets.

And a Christmas feast came a few days early that year.

* * *

After washing up in the bathroom, Joey stared into the empty mirror and unleashed a rank blood burp. He took the stack of "Gotta read" comics from the boy's bedroom that he drained earlier that evening and headed down to into the dark, windowless basement. Dawn was approaching and he wanted to get a little bedtime reading in before hitting the sack. Then he would get a good day's rest since he had a big night planned for later. With his creepy competitor out of the way, little Joey now had his pick of the litter when it came to the neighborhood families that he could have for dinner.

Santa's CARNIVAL of Blood Dusk till Dawn Slayathon

ROBERT FREESE

Story Art Cover
By David Naughton-Shires
http://www.TheImageDesigns.com

Dedication
To the loving memory of my wife Frances and all the wonderful Christmases we shared.

Author Bio
Robert Freese is the author of the zombie novel **Bijou of the Dead** as well as the horror/sci-fi novella **The Santa Thing** (both from Stone-Garden.net Publishing). He co-wrote **Paranormal Journeys** with paranormal investigator Paul Cagle (also from StoneGarden.net Publishing). His short horror story collection, **Shivers**, is available through eTreasures Publishing. StoneGarden.net Publishing will release his forthcoming collection **13 Frights** in 2012. His most recent stories have appeared in CD Publications' **In Laymon's Terms**, the NorGus Press anthologies **Strange Tales of Horror** and **Look What I Found!** and the Pill Hill Press anthology **Daily Bites of Flesh: 2011**. In addition, Robert contributes regularly to **The Phantom of the Movies' Videoscope Magazine** and **Scary Monsters Magazine**.

Santa's Carnival of Blood Dusk till Dawn Slayathon
By Robert Freese

That crazy chick bit me!

At the entrance of Duffy's Tavern, Derek Chambers leaned against the door. He was clutching his neck, wetness seeping between his fingers. Daring to look, he stared at his blood covering the palm of his hand and finger tips.

"Crap." He put his hand back on the wound on his neck. It throbbed horribly. Who knows what kind of diseases could be spread from biting?

Suddenly he felt lightheaded, like he was a little drunk, but he had barely had anything to drink before the black haired chick started hitting on him. Before he knew it, they were dancing, and then in a booth in one of the tavern's dark corners. She was all over him, encouraging him to put his hands all over her. Derek had his hand up her skirt and she purred with delight.

Then she bit me!

Did he go to the hospital? It was Christmas Eve. The emergency room would be full of drunks and accident victims. He had to get home. Fishing in his front pocket for his car keys he pulled them free only to drop them on the gravel lot. Someone in high heels approached him from behind.

"Where are you going, lover? We were just getting started," the raven haired beauty purred.

"Get away from me." Snatching up the keys, moving too fast and nearly falling, Derek leaned against the tavern wall and made his way to the parking lot. The lot was full and it took him what seemed several long minutes to find his car. The entire time the woman watched and giggled from the tavern's front entrance.

Did she even give you her name? Kelly? Kelly what? If you do go to the hospital, you'll have to tell them who bit you.

He was feeling sicker now, worrying about the bite becoming infected or worse, contracting some disease. It was obvious the woman had done that before. Maybe even tonight! Maybe she had some other dude's skin or blood between her teeth. Derek's gorge began rising at the sickening thought. Finding his car he unlocked the door with considerable effort and slumped into the driver's seat.

Is it hot in here or is it just me? It was an unseasonably warm Christmas Eve night, even for the south.

Is it a fever? Am I getting sick already?

Starting the car he jumped into gear and lurched forward, almost smacking into a car pulling out in front of him. The other driver honked and waved a fist in his direction.

Derek threw up his hands and the other driver went on. When it was clear he pulled out of the tavern's parking lot.

Laughing, Kelly was joined by a brunette and a redhead. The redhead, Stacey, was wiping a crimson splash from her chin. "I love the holidays," she said and all three women laughed.

Teresa, the brunette, turned to Kelly and said, "Go get Barbie. I think we're going hunting tonight." The raven haired woman laughed and went back into Duffy's to find the blonde.

* * *

Derek felt his heartbeat thumping wildly in the wound on his neck and throughout his skull. There was no doubt about it; he wouldn't make it to the hospital. He was going to throw up or pass out first. He needed to pull over. There was nothing around for miles. The tavern was more like an out of the way roadhouse on the outskirts of town. The only other place this far out in the middle of nowhere was...

Then he saw the giant marquee glowing brightly in the winter darkness. A rocket ship swooped around the underside of the marquee and up the side, leaving a slipstream of colorful neon beams behind. The theater's name, The Cosmic Drive-in, stood out atop the sign in bright red neon. The marquee read: Santa's Carnival of Blood Dusk till Dawn Slayathon and below that the titles of five movies; "Dead Christmas", "Evil Elves", "Silent Night, Violent Night", "Toy Store Massacre", and "Murder Claus". Below the titles was the line, "Yule Scream with Terror from this All Nite Fright!"

Derek had nowhere else to go. It was five dollars a carload. He could use the restroom to clean the wound and get it to stop bleeding. He could rest a minute and then call Lenny or

Dale to ride out and pick him up. That crazy, crazy chick! *Why did she have to bite me?*

* * *

Wayne entered the snack bar carrying the metal till box from the box office. Evelyn was behind the counter filling a large popcorn tub and two large soda cups for a young couple. Her smile was the brightest, most genuine smile he had ever seen, and he stood quietly, basking in its glow, as she covered the fluffy kernels with red dyed butter. "Blood Corn" was tonight's specialty to go along with the all night horror show.

She was a natural beauty. He didn't think she wore much make-up except for a little blush on her cheeks and a light colored lipstick on her lips. Her blue-grey eyes sparkled, like they forever hid some wonderful secret behind them. Blonde with dark highlights and naturally wavy, her hair was pulled back in a ponytail that trailed down her back. She was slim, petite, but not skinny. Her body was shapely with nice curves in the best places. Wayne had been completely smitten by her the moment Kenny introduced her to him two weeks ago when he hired her on as temporary help over the six weeks Mrs. Margret, the older woman who usually manned the snack bar, went down to visit her son and his family in Florida for the winter.

The weekend earlier he had helped Evelyn decorate a fake Christmas tree that looked to be older than Kenny, the drive-in's long time projectionist and owner. It smelled stale after being tucked away in the storage room all year and Wayne had worried that there might be mice nesting in the wire branches, but luckily there weren't. He and Evelyn came in early to set it up and decorate it with empty candy boxes, small popcorn bags and old promotional items they found in a box in the storage room like 3-D glasses, gimmick vomit bags and other such items. Evelyn even got creative and made a string of garland from an old roll of tickets. The tree blended perfectly in the snack bar.

He had hoped to learn a little about her while they decorated the tree, like if she had a boyfriend, or someone she was interested in back at the college, but they had spent most of their time laughing and joking around. He kept taping candy boxes on her back and she retaliated every time. Twice Kenny had to tell them to decorate the tree, not each other. They just laughed. It was easy to laugh with Evelyn, she had one of the most magnificent smiles and rosy cheeks. Ultimately, all he had learned was that she was home from college for a few weeks and she needed to work as much as she could to earn money for the Spring semester's books she needed, which was the only thing her limited scholarship didn't cover. Working at the old drive-in was the only job she could find when she returned home after her finals earlier in the month.

After the boy paid and the couple was gone Wayne sauntered up to the glass display case where the variety of candies were laid out and dropped the metal till on the glass top with a clank.

"Hey you," Evelyn said with a smile.

"Is it hopping in here or what?"

"Not too bad. Looks like about a dozen cars or so," she said, looking out the picture window to the lot. The giant outdoor screen was crackling to life with the first feature in the horrothon.

"Yeah, a lot more than what I expected for a Christmas Eve. Most of them are single people who don't have anywhere else to go. The kids like those last two will probably split after the second movie or so." He ran his fingers through his hair, a habit he picked up in high school when he felt nervous talking to a female. "Man, you should have seen the last geek that came through. Sweaty, bloodshot eyes, he looked like he was coming off a five day drunk."

Still smiling, Evelyn said, "He's probably trying to sober up before going home to the wife and kids. I'll make a fresh pot of coffee in case he wanders in here." She had a damp cloth and was wiping down the display's glass top. Wayne picked up the till and moved it out of her way.

"I guess. I still think it's insane to be opened on Christmas Eve. Every year we are open for a 'dusk to dawn' show on Christmas Eve and I wonder why anyone would want to be here." He went around to the back side of the counter.

"At least it's a nice night," she said. She had a way of always finding something positive to say.

"Yeah, but there'll be no white Christmas for us this year."

"I'd love to have a white Christmas," she said with a sigh. "Anyway, like I told you, I have to have money for books or I won't be able to take a full semester in the spring. If I can't take a full load, I may lose my scholarship."

"Yeah, I'm just trying to earn enough to get my own place come the first of the year." As soon as he said it he wished he could hit rewind and go back five seconds.

Dumb! Way to go, Slick. No better way to announce what a geek you are to a girl you like than admitting that you're still living with your parents.

It wasn't like he was forty still living with them. He was only twenty, the same age as Evelyn, but he felt like a kid around her. She seemed so much older and worldly than he did. Maybe because she was away at college and was doing something with her life and he was still working at The Cosmic Drive-in after four years, not doing anything different with his life than he did when he was sixteen.

She said, "That's cool. It's hard to move out. I'm scared about when I finish school in the fall. My dad already turned my old bedroom into his college football room, so there's no moving back home with them. I mean, maybe for a while I can sleep on the couch, but I'll have to find a place pretty quick. Maybe you'll be able to help me out." Then that smile again.

"Sure." He felt like a goofball. But she was so easy to talk to, like they'd known each other forever. Truth be told, he only agreed to work the Christmas Eve dusk till dawn show because she was working it. It had really upset his mom, as they had a family custom of going out to eat on Christmas Eve after Mass and then going home and everybody opened one gift from under the tree. He intended to move out soon, even though his parents weren't pushing him, but Kenny was paying time and a half for working the holiday shift, so that would help. He assured his mom he would be home in the morning in time to open presents with Davy and Danielle, his little brother and sister. He went around the counter to her side.

He pressed the red button on the ancient intercom system and buzzed the projection booth. Kenny came on. His voice was broken by bursts of static and random pops.

"I got the box office locked up." Wayne took his finger off

the button to await a reply.

"Did you remember to put the sign in the box office window?" Wayne mouthed the older man's response perfectly. Evelyn giggled. It was the same question the owner had asked every night Wayne had worked over the last four years.

"Yes, sir, the sign is in the window." The yellow placard directed any late coming patrons to the box office to purchase a ticket once the ticket booth was closed.

"Good. Come get the office key and lock up the till box."

"Roger that, good buddy. Ten-four. Over and out." He clicked off the intercom. To the girl he said in his best impersonation of Arnold Schwarzenegger, "I'll be back." Evelyn giggled again, her face lighting up with her smile. She watched him leave through the back entrance, which lead up to the projection booth.

* * *

The white '59 convertible Thunderbird blasted down the highway like a wild boar tearing through jungle foliage. It ate the dark miles with an engine roar that sounded like a freshly awakened hell-beast. Warm night air blew through the hair of the four young women in the car.

"I smell him," Kelly said with a smile. She looked hungry. Her hands gripped the steering wheel tightly.

"I sense something," Barbie, the blonde, started. Her lids closed and she seemed to concentrate on an overwhelming feeling filling her being. "A presence I haven't felt since..." Her words tapered off into the night. A memory suddenly came to her, her red lips curling into a cruel smile.

The darkness gave way to glowing neon brilliance. There was a fantastic burst of colorful light as the marquee for the Cosmic Drive-in came into view.

"You've got to be kidding me," Barbie said with a laugh.

"You know the place?" Teresa, the brunette, asked from the backseat.

"Know it? This is where I was re-born, girls. I didn't even know that junky old passion pit was still open." She laughed again. "Step on it."

Kelly stomped on the accelerator and the T-Bird jumped

forward, its engine howling, screeching, as the final miles were quickly consumed.

* * *

Derek was sick. There was a gnawing hunger in his gut. His body felt like it was on fire.

She made me sick! That crazy chick gave me a disease or virus, something bad!

Rolling down his window for some fresh air, the warm night breeze blew over him. It did little to help. On the giant screen a blood splashed Santa Claus was frantically reloading a shotgun as zombie elves pushed through a barricade. Santa snapped the double barrel shotgun in time to fire off both rounds into the heads of the two closest of the rushing miniature undead. The monsters' heads exploded like chunky sugar plums in a splash of red and white gore. There were several appreciative honks from the various patrons around the lot. Derek was not paying any attention to the film. He was looking at the nearest car to him.

Three spaces over was a young couple. The boy had been one of the patrons who honked his horn. The girl hid her eyes from the gory scene on the screen, but she was smiling and laughing with the boy. They munched contentedly from the large popcorn tub between them.

Derek's mouth began to water. Not from the popcorn, or the crimson colored butter that covered it, but from the girl's exposed neck. He could smell the blood coursing through her veins. The salty, coppery taste tempted his gnawing urge to feed.

All he would have to do was reach through the open window, grab her by the hair and jerk her head out the window. She wouldn't know what was going on until it was too late, until he had already exposed her vulnerable neck and bit deeply into her. Her blood would be pouring down his throat before her boyfriend even knew what happened. The gnawing hunger would be sated, he would somehow be better.

What is wrong with me?

* * *

Stacey, the redhead, entered the snack bar with Barbie. Evelyn smiled but even before she greeted the girls she felt a chill run down her spine.

The redhead smiled back at her. "You're pretty."

Evelyn didn't know what to say but tried not to let her smile waver. "Did you need a ticket for the show?" She tried to sound chipper, but she could hear her voice crack.

"Why not," the blonde said, sizing the girl behind the glass counter up.

"It's five dollars a carload." She couldn't say why, but these two girls, women when she really looked into their eyes, scared her.

"What a deal," the blonde said with a laugh. The redhead took a roll of bills out of her purse and peeled off a hundred dollar bill. She flicked it at the counter where it fluttered to the glass top like a bird with two broken wings.

"I don't think I have enough change to break this," Evelyn said. She picked it up to hand it back to the redhead.

"Keep it," Barbie said. Her red painted lips seemed to stretch to an almost grotesque point.

"Okay," Evelyn said, putting the money in the register. She slid them a ticket. The blonde picked it up and said, "A souvenir." She laughed.

Before they left the redhead motioned toward the hand written sign Evelyn had made earlier and asked, "What is 'Blood Corn'?"

"It's just popcorn with butter that has been dyed red." Evelyn's voice suddenly sounded so small and insignificant.

"Oh, so it's not real blood? What a shame. Never mind then." She turned to leave.

"See you later, sweetie," the blonde said with a lick of her lips and a wink, following the redhead out of the snack bar.

* * *

Moving with a stealth he had never before possessed, the new hunger burning in the pit of his stomach, Derek crept toward the nearby young couple. Unaware of his presence they munched contentedly on their snacks, watching the movie as it played toward its conclusion.

Each step was carefully placed so as not to offer any telltale noise of his approach. He moved lightly on the gravel. Sweat poured down his forehead and back. His muscles were starting to twitch uncontrollably. His body was beginning to ache horribly.

When he was close enough to the open car window the scent of the girl's pumping blood was so overwhelming he thought he would double over in excruciating pain if he did not feed immediately. He reached for her.

"What are you doing, lover?"

The voice was smooth, like silk, and danced on the warm night wind. Jerking his arm away, he took a clumsy step away from the car and saw the dark haired girl from Duffy's. She was smiling seductively.

The girl in the car was now aware of his presence and screamed in surprise. Her boyfriend swore and quickly got out of his car to see what was happening.

Kelly's wicked smile did not falter. "You must be getting hungry, lover. You're just going to have to wait until we finish feeding." She licked her lips.

"Seriously, what the hell is going on?" the boy repeated. "Is this some kind of Christmas lover's quarrel, because if it is, you need to take it to back to your car and away from here, okay? We're trying to watch the movie." He looked angry, his hands balled into fists. His girlfriend had rolled up her window.

Suddenly, the darkness was alive. Stacey swooped in and grabbed the boy from behind. Her razor sharp fangs pierced his neck as he screamed.

Inside the car, the girl screamed again. The sound of shattering glass permeated the night. A storm of pebbled glass rained down on the girl as she was dragged out through the smashed window. Kelly moved quickly to bite into the girl's exposed neck.

"Feed," Barbie exclaimed to her girls. "Feed on them all! It's a Christmas buffet!" Her laugh was like thunder and it echoed eerily in the night.

The vampire women went from car to car, feasting on the blood of the inhabitants, spreading their fast acting blood virus. Careful not to fully drain anyone, each person they bit would instantly become infected. Those infected would then have to feed to become full vampires.

People ran from their vehicles to the snack bar. Some were cut down and bitten, left rolling on the ground in agony, but a few made it to safety.

Evelyn didn't know what was going on but she heard enough from the scared patrons to lock the snack bar doors. All they could do was watch through the big picture window as the vampire women continued their vicious attack. Slowly, bodies jerking as if on strings, their victims stood and joined them, a blood hunger gnawing away at them. When the last patron had been pierced like a juice box and fed on, the vampire women turned their attention to the snack bar. Barbie smiled.

How appropriate. The snack bar.

The end credits flickered on the big screen. There was a scratch and pop that spat from the speakers all over the lot and then the next movie started up without missing a beat.

* * *

Kenny had been paying little attention to the comings and goings down on the lot while changing the movie reels and remembering a different time in his life. When he was alone in his projection booth, he looked back at the fifty-two years he'd stayed at The Cosmic Drive-in, lost in the memories of showing movies on the big screen. Since he was eighteen, his life had not changed one bit. Now he was seventy and still the only future he saw for himself was changing reels for the next double feature or dusk to dawn show.

He had worked hard, saved enough money to buy the theater from Mr. Barnett when he wanted to retire with his wife Sherry back in the early seventies. The theater did well throughout the seventies and into the eighties, but it had made little sense to keep it open the last twenty years. But it was the only life he had ever known. When local developers threatened to seize the property, enough people rallied to have the old drive-in declared a historical site, thus extending its life a little longer, until the legal gangsters could finagle another way of stealing the property away.

His life had never been the same after that summer of '59.

How his life would have been different he could not rightly say, but he knew it would have been different. Obviously, he would have married, probably had children and now he would possibly be a grandfather if not a great grandfather. But sometimes life had different plans for you than you had for yourself. He adjusted to his new life, even if he hated every second he had lived from that point on.

So, after watching that life he had so dearly desired perish before his eyes, he stopped living. He became a ghost and had spent the last fifty-two years of his life haunting the Cosmic Drive-in.

Lost in his thoughts, paying little attention to the outside world, he took a moment to look out the projection booth window at the cars below. For years he had been offering the Christmas Eve dusk to dawn show for the lost and the lonely. There was never a year when people didn't show up. Then he saw it, his heart skipping a beat.

The white 1959 Ford Thunderbird Convertible. It looked exactly like he remembered it. The last time he saw it he had been covered in blood and the T-Bird was screeching from the lot, never to be seen again until tonight.

He scanned the lot and saw the chaos. It had never been like this before, people being attacked in the open. All the blood. Then he saw them, the pack of wild women, Stacey, Kelly and Teresa. Blood was dripping from their lips.

Why were they back? Why tonight? His mind was ablaze with questions. *Where was...*

The thought was cut off when he saw her. She was strolling up the center of the lot, her minions falling in behind her. They were moving toward the snack bar.

The snack bar!

Kenny started up the next movie in the Christmas Eve horrothon. Never let it be said that he ever missed a reel, not even the last one.

Grabbing the satchel he kept hidden beneath the editing table where he spliced damaged prints, he shuffled out of the projection booth, knowing that he would probably never return to play another reel ever again. But that was okay. Sometimes life had different plans for you than you had for yourself.

* * *

In the commotion, Wayne made his way to where Evelyn was locking the doors. Hearing screaming from the lot while he locked up the till in the office, he had hurried to get back to the snack bar to check on Evelyn.

"What are they?" Evelyn asked. She was scared. She moved close to Wayne. He dared put a protective arm around her. She felt good, warm.

"Blood dripping fangs, people with bite marks on their necks..." His voice sort of tapered off.

"Don't say it," she said.

"What else could they be?"

The first of the infected minions slammed against the snack bar's giant picture window. The females in the snack bar all screamed with fright.

Behind the vampires, the screen was alive with the second movie of the fright show. The action had already started in the opening moments as an insane Santa Claus drove an oversized sharpened candy cane through the heads of two teenagers parked in a 'Lover's Lane.' The laugh from the maniacal Santa echoed throughout the speakers on the lot. It was a surreal moment, the crazy movie on the big screen at the back end of the lot with the approaching bloodsuckers stalking closer in the foreground.

"What do we do?" Evelyn looked to Wayne. He didn't know what to say.

"Get away from the glass." The voice was loud and commanding. Everyone turned toward the back of the snack bar. It was Kenny. He sounded different, more authoritative than usual. He laid a black satchel on the glass display top after locking the door behind him.

"If they break the glass, and they will, you'll be the first two they snatch," he said directly to his employees. The others in the snack bar had crowded against the far wall, near the ancient pinball machines and video games.

"Quickly," Kenny said to the nearest people, "fill as many cups as you can with soda. Half full is fine." He opened the satchel.

"What is going on?" Wayne asked. He helped separate cups

while Evelyn and a couple of the others filled them and placed them on the counter.

"Vampires," Kenny said matter-of-factly.

"Vampires. Seriously?"

"Yes, seriously," the older man answered. "I've been dealing with them for fifty-two years." He took out a crossbow and then a silver cross.

"Vampires," Wayne repeated.

"Yes, Wayne, vampires. They only come out at night. This is a drive-in movie theater. We are only open at night. We've had plenty of vampires come through here over the years who tried to make snacks of our patrons. You've sold tickets to many of them. Every so often there's that abandoned car." He looked over and saw two dozen drink cups on the counter. He said, "That's good." Holding out his hand over the paper cups he silently recited a prayer. Then he said, "When they break in here, and they will break in here, you throw these sodas on them. It won't kill them, but it will burn them, make them run away for a minute."

"You just blessed all those sodas?" Wayne asked, disbelieving.

"That's right." The older man quickly bowed an arrow into the crossbow.

"Holy sodas?"

"Any liquid will do. I had to use a wine cooler one time back in the 80s."

"Are you a priest or something?"

"Something like that. I was ordained years ago. I did it by a correspondence course through the mail. I got a certificate and everything. I guess today you kids would do all that through the Interweb, but back then we did it by mail. Stamps were four cents back then."

The minions were beating on the window glass. They were making a heck of a ruckus but it would be a little while before they broke through. Two were at the back entrance now, pulling at the glass door.

"I need everyone to listen," Kenny said in a booming voice. "I know this doesn't seem real, but trust me, it is. Usually there's only an occasional vampire who wanders onto the lot looking for a quick snack, but tonight we've got a pack. These people from the cars, they are not vampires. Not until they feed. They get one of you and feed, they'll turn. Those four girls out there, they're the real deal. Each of them is as old as your grandmas. Don't be fooled by them. The blonde is the leader. We stake the leader, the people bitten out there will be saved. Does everyone understand?"

The patrons just stared open eyed and scared. The pounding on the window glass was booming.

"Does everyone understand?"

There were a few weak replies, which was enough for the old man. "Good. Watch your necks, help each other and watch you don't slip on any glass when they break through. Now everyone grab two of the sodas." The scared patrons did as they were told.

"Uh, question," Wayne said, raising his hand like he was in school again. "You seem to know those, uh, ladies out there. Care to elaborate?"

Kenny wistfully looked out at the blonde, the leader of the pack of vampire women. Old feelings and memories stirred within him. Love could be cruel. Instead of saying any of this, he said, "Just know they're bad news and they're tougher than they look. But the blessed sodas will work on them too. You leave them to me."

"Great," the boy mumbled.

"Wayne, I'm scared." Evelyn was holding on to him.

"I wish I was only scared. There's a good chance I'm going to crap my pants." He looked into the girl's eyes. Even frightened they sparkled with mystery. "Just stick close to me." He handed her two of the half filled paper cups. He turned to where the theater owner had been standing, but the old man was gone.

"He must have ducked into the storage room," Evelyn said. The two-way door between the snack bar proper and the short hallway back to the storage room was still swinging gently on its rusted hinges.

* * *

In the storage room Kenny moved some boxes and then unlocked a hidden door. Outside it was warm, downright humid for late December. He locked the door behind him. He moved with a stealth that easily betrayed his years. Walking cautiously on the gravel lot, he came around the side of the building. He raised the crossbow and aimed.

* * *

"Look!" Evelyn pointed outside, just past the glass banging pseudo-vamps. The blonde saw her pointing finger and looked to her left. Kenny fired the crossbow. The wooden tipped arrow whizzed through the air like an angry hornet.

Stacey, the redhead, stopped and shrieked wildly. The arrow pierced her heart. She had just long enough to look over at the man who killed her and then her eyes blew out of her skull with a volcanic rush of fire. Her head ignited, exploding in a brilliant bright white light, followed by her heart and the rest of her body. The only thing left of her was a memory as even the ashes of her body incinerated into nothing.

"Get him!" Barbie hissed. The old man was gone, but Teresa and Kelly chased after him.

* * *

"Did you see that?" Evelyn's eyes were as wide as pie plates.

"Evelyn!" Wayne grabbed for the girl, pulled her away from the giant window before a brick shattered it into a million jagged pieces. It cracked like thunder followed by a rainstorm of glass shards. There were screams but many of the patrons were quick to toss the blessed colas at the line of oncoming vamps-in-training.

The soda hit them in the face with a fizzle. After a moment the vampire minions were screaming wildly, smoke rising from their burning faces and then the fizzle sound gave way to a wicked sizzle, much like a hot dog on the grill.

"What are you doing?" Barbie snapped at the minions. Those not fully splashed had backed away, afraid after seeing what happened to those on the front line.

* * *

111

Teresa and Kelly were moving as quick as the warm night breeze, but they could not find the old man. Teresa sniffed the air, caught a trace of her prey and immediately looked up to the roof of the snack bar. She noticed the ladder bolted to the side of the building a couple feet away. A demonic smile stretched across her grotesque features. Smiling, she made a mighty leap and landed on the roof. Kelly followed.

Out of breath and wheezing uncontrollably, the old man was leaning against the side wall of the air conditioning unit. One hand was gripping his heart, as if trying to prevent it from bursting from his chest. His eyes were full of terror as the vampire women approached.

"You stupid, old fool! You shouldn't have killed Stacey," Kelly said through gritted fangs.

"We're going to make you suffer," Teresa added. "Your suffering will go down in history. Robert Ripley wouldn't believe it. We're going to keep you alive for a hundred years and each day will be worse than the last."

"A lot of talk," Kenny said between gasps of air. "That's all you monsters know how to do beside spread your awful disease." He was red faced and looked like he could be having a stroke or a heart attack or a little bit of both.

"Pain, old man, is the disease. And you're about five seconds from being swallowed up by it. You'll pray for death every day, but all you'll receive is more pain." With that Kelly made her move, swooping in on him as if on invisible wings. Her fangs bared; as soon as she was face to face with the old man, about to bite deep into his neck, he moved.

The hand over his heart grabbed a handful of her raven tresses and jerked her head back. She hissed and tried to free herself, but his grip on her was like steel. Before she could break loose his other hand appeared from the shadows. Clutching a container of Mama London's Zesty Powdered Garlic Mix he shoved the open end into the vampire's wide mouth. The powdered mixture of garlic and spices, the real secret behind the drive-in's famous pizza and meatball sandwiches, poured down the bloodsucker's throat.

Working immediately, the garlic powder began dissolving everything it touched, like acid. Kenny released her. Stumbling backwards, Kelly grabbed at her throat. She opened her mouth to scream but instead a chunky wave of pus, goo and blood came pouring out. Liquefied internal organs soon followed, splashing the roof with a hiss like raw hamburger on the grill.

What she didn't expel from her mouth came pouring out holes in her stomach, the garlic powder eating away her flesh. Gooey ropes of intestines gushed out and liquefied when they hit the rooftop. It was like a chink in a dam giving way to a gory flood.

Gagging, gasping, agony filling her eyes until her head began dissolving away from the mouth up, Kelly melted like the wicked witch in "The Wizard of Oz". Within seconds of swallowing the powder, the raven haired vampire was a bubbling puddle of snot, goo and blood.

"Kelly!" Teresa had no time to act. She was stunned, having never seen one of her kind killed before. Her eyes, cut into vengeful slits, turned down on Kenny.

"Screw suffering! I'm going to rip out your heart and feed it to you!"

"Stop, you creature of the night!" Kenny bellowed dramatically. From his satchel he withdrew the metal crucifix and held it at arm's length. Moonlight glinted off the silver cross.

Teresa laughed. "You are a pathetic, ignorant old man. Crucifixes only work if I believe in God. I'm not like the minions. You shouldn't believe every stupid thing you see in the movies."

"Then I pray for your soul, foolish girl. But believe me when I say God believes in you." Moving fluidly, Kenny flipped his wrist and expertly threw the cross like a dagger. It seemed to tumble through the air in slow motion, speeding up only when closing in on its target, entering Teresa's chest and piercing her heart.

Eyes wide with horror and pain, she looked at the top of the crucifix protruding from her chest. For a moment she saw her reflection on its shiny, polished surface. Pain was erupting from where the sharpened point had burst through her back.

"I thought it had to be wood," she said in a tiny voice.

"You shouldn't believe every stupid thing you see in the movies."

The silver crucifix glowed brightly, burning like a supernova. Smoke poured from around the wound. Teresa opened her mouth to scream but was devoured in a brilliant burst of fire as her body was completely consumed from the inside out.

When it was over, the cross clanked onto the rooftop. The air smelled of burnt flesh and hair.

Grabbing the crucifix first, Kenny hefted his body up and got moving to join the others.

* * *

Barbie pushed past her minions and lunged for the shattered picture window into the snack bar. Her eyes glowed demonically, her features transforming into a hell spawn, her fangs huge and dagger-like.

She stopped her rampage when Evelyn splashed the last cup of blessed holy soda into her face. Her face sizzled, pustules bubbling, bursting and spewing thick, yellow ooze. Unlike the others, this did not seem to faze the vampire woman. In a moment the sores and burned skin healed and her features, although grotesque, were back to normal.

"You're starting to bug me, girlfriend." Barbie struck out, hitting Evelyn and knocking her into the Christmas tree. She crumbled to the floor.

"Hey!" Wayne rushed toward the blond vampire unarmed. Before he could reach her she lashed out and grabbed him around the neck. Picking him up off the floor with ease, his legs kicking uselessly, Barbie dragged him outside and bit deeply into his neck.

She drank long, delighting on the boy's sanguinary sustenance. The blond night creature left just enough blood in him so the boy would live, but her virus would be passed on to him. She dropped his body onto the snack bar floor.

Pain filled his every nerve ending. Wayne was dizzy. He felt both nauseous and hungry. He had never before experienced such an intense hunger. It drove him, forced him to get up. He could smell what he craved in the people trapped inside the snack bar. Blood flowed through each of them. Then desire overtook him. He wanted the girl. Evelyn. Before he could snatch her, drink from her neck, she ran past him.

"You miserable, monster-bitch!" Evelyn rushed the vampire with a jagged branch from the artificial tree. Empty boxes of chocolate covered almonds, licorice strings, gummy slugs and Up Chuck Cups dangled from the branch. She jammed the metal end into Barbie's heart, shoving it deep, right up to a dangling box of Vanilla Wingdingers.

Shocked, the vampire woman stumbled away from the window a couple steps. She looked down and saw the artificial Christmas tree branch that seemed to be growing from her chest. The minions watched, hunched and frightened around her. Her look of shock turned into the most monstrous smile any of them had ever seen. When she spoke, her voice was deep, taking on a demonic timbre.

"This won't work on me, girlfriend. Not from you. I'm going to make slaves of you all." Grabbing the wire tree branch, Barbie ripped it from her chest. It made a sucking noise. The point dripped black blood.

"But it will work for me!" Kenny was suddenly there. He had an old school wooden stake and he plunged it deep into Barbie's dead black heart.

"Kenny!" She looked stunned. Pain inflicted her entire being. Then her features softened. "What happened to you? You got so old." Her voice sounded like a teenage girl again.

"I've waited for this night for fifty-two years, baby. I knew you'd come back to me sooner or later."

A tear rolled down her cheek. "I missed you. Why didn't you come with me?"

"And live like a monster? Not my style Barb. Not yours either."

"I'm cold, Kenny. Hold me."

"I'm right here." Even though he felt her body turning to ice the old man held her tightly. "You're still as beautiful as I remember."

"You really waited for me all these years?" Her tears were turning to ice on her cheeks and chin.

Now tears were streaming down Kenny's face. "I never loved anyone else. I always loved just you."

Something in her eyes changed. The monster inside was gone. Now she was just the girl he had fallen in love with so many years ago.

They embraced. The temperature around the drive-in dropped drastically. A bright light began emanating from the

Robert Freese

hole in Barbie's chest, around the stake. Kenny never let her go. He glanced over at Evelyn and Wayne, could tell the boy was changing back with the rest of them, and he gave them a knowing wink.

They glowed brightly for a moment before exploding together in brilliant strike of icy cold lightning that left a darkened pit on the lot where they were standing. The wind whirled wildly and a crack of thunder pierced the air and another blast of lightning struck the ground. Everyone screamed as an arctic wind blew through and the first flakes of snow started falling.

Evelyn helped Wayne to his feet. Everyone else was wandering around in a daze. Those who had been bitten no longer carried the vampire virus. The leader of the pack had been destroyed, destroyed by the one person who truly loved her.

The flakes were swirling wildly and people began going to their cars. Dawn was still several hours away. As they drove away they realized it was only snowing on the lot of The Cosmic Drive-in.

"I need to tell you something," Wayne said as he limped over to the counter. The vampire virus was gone, but he still felt weak from losing so much blood. He needed some kind of candy. "I only agreed to work tonight because Kenny said you were working."

Evelyn smiled brightly.

"What?" he asked, opening a box of Chocolate Snickerdoodles.

"I only agreed to work tonight because Kenny said you were working."

"I thought you needed money for books."

"Sure, but who wants to work on Christmas Eve? I just wanted to get to know you."

"Well smack my butt and call me Bunky," he said. She laughed. "I learned a lot about you tonight."

"What did you learn?" she asked, helping him walk to the snack bar exit.

"I learned you're a tough chick who will bitch-slap a vampire down without thinking about herself."

Evelyn laughed.

Outside snow blew around them and they held each other close.

116

"You got your white Christmas," Wayne said, looking up into the falling flakes.

"It's beautiful."

"Let's grab something to eat. Maybe some chicken and waffles?"

"Sounds delicious," she said with that wonderful, marvelous smile.

"I got to do something first," he said, stopping.

"Do we need to lock up? Call the cops?"

"Naw, just this." He grabbed her and pulled her close. Their lips met. An electric current of warmth buzzed gently between them. They held like that a long moment before breaking free.

"You're one heck of a kisser," she said with a laugh and a smile.

"I practice on the mirror at home all the time."

"Really?" Her smile was glowing.

"Drives my roommates crazy when the mirror is always smudged."

"Roommates?"

"Yeah, they're like parents to me they've been so good to me over the years."

Evelyn laughed and helped him over to where their cars were parked. She helped him into her little VW convertible bug. The top was down. "I'll drive tonight. We'll come back and get your car later."

"Sounds like a deal. You can pay for dinner too if you want to."

"I need my money for school books, remember?"

Smiling, he leaned over and kissed her again. It was a kiss they felt for the rest of their lives. A fat snowflake landed gently upon their lips and melted, binding them together.

They drove away, leaving the Cosmic Drive-in behind for the moment, the snow covering every inch of the lot as Kenny and Barbie watched from beyond.

SUCCESSION PLANNING

DAMON B

Story Art Cover
By David Naughton-Shires
http://www.TheImageDesigns.com

Dedication

To the beautiful and sometimes desolate landscapes that inspired me - kayaking in the Archipelago off the coast of Norköpping, and road trips through the Outback and along the cliffs of the Eyre Peninsula.

Author Bio

Damon B is an Antipodean creature who roams the world and drives out the tedium of a daytime desk job with tales of the undead, tattoo cults, and life after the Apocalypse. He also feature online at Macabre Cadaver with his piece "Inkorporated", and in the Rigor Amortis anthology with "Liberation Den".

Succession Planning
By Damon B

Something had gone wrong, and now He was missing.

It had been known to happen. Sometimes, someone went insane upon Turning, and usually Karl-Heinz's family dealt with such incidents with a quiet "abortion" a swift beheading of the malformed undead, or sometimes a staking. That just wouldn't do in this case, though. Not for Klaus. They couldn't just dispose of him without someone noticing, and they couldn't command the respect of the elves with some impostor. For all his family's centuries of wisdom in helping Popes and Mafioso ascend their thrones, Karl-Heinz had to admit that he still had no damned idea how Klaus actually delivered all those presents in one night.

And now Klaus had disappeared. None of the hundreds of elves had seen him in weeks, nor had packs of huskies succeeded in tracking him across the tundra. All they had to go on were old reports from the northern Finnish planes and Swedish coast of a wild-eyed, bearded fiend savaging backpackers, reindeer and red squirrels.

Shit, it's the second of December and we have a bloody PR disaster on our hands.

* * *

It was the height of summer, when the drought-stricken Australian bush lay thirsty and fractured beneath a brutal sun, and the Murray River was a parched thread in the landscape, so shallow in parts that ferries were useless and only kayaks could navigate stretches.

He had already smelled their delicious odour from a good two hundred meters away as he shambled along the riverbank, and now he was observing the campsite from a nearby thicket. The unwashed campers were dozing in a humid little tent close to the bank, with swarms of sand flies and mozzies menacing the canvas tent hull and the unwashed dishes discarded around the cold campfire.

Like the kamikaze mozzies, the scent of all that live flesh, of healthy hearts pumping hot blood, was driving him to nearly unbearable craving and blind, hungering instinct; but some remnant of cunning, those skills he'd used for over a century to skulk into countless houses, stayed his body in the dry grass, fingers and mouth biting into the gritty soil to stop his moaning and fidgeting.

The sounds of sleeping were deep and even, and his body shuddered with delight as he crawled from the fringe of trees where the campers had earlier shovelled their toilet. Cautiously crawling forward a few metres more, his fat belly was crushing the soil and lantana grass tufts as he stopped beneath the line of dripping t-shirts and board shorts that were strung on old fishing line between a couple of stunted eucalypts at the edge of the clearing. A red towel on the line briefly stirred a memory of red cloth covering his body, and a name echoed in his skull for a second: Klaus.

A large sea-worthy kayak was pulled up on to the reeds off to the side, and he could smell week old vegetables and Devon ham spoiling in the hull. That meat wouldn't do at all for his hunger. He'd already discovered that his cravings couldn't be staved by the corpse of a pensioner he'd found on the bank a day ago (or was it even a week ago?), a loner he'd simply found lying by his easel, brush still gripped in one hand.

A sudden clattering of hooves and Klaus whipped his head to the right. About fifteen metres further along the shore was a shoulder of rock rising out of the river and forming one wing of the natural harbour. A dozen scruffy sheep had emerged. A couple of rams kept a lookout in the direction of the tent, while the others bent their heads to the water's edge.

His stomach grumbled, and a moan escaped his lips this time. So much food, so close.

The sheep had all turned toward his moaning and seen him. In another clatter of hooves they were racing among the brush. He raised himself to race in pursuit, but then the breeze came from the direction of the tent, carrying the scent of the cooling ashes in the fireplace and of the sweaty bodies beneath the canvas. This was so much more addictive than the wool-shrouded forms.

He circled the tent on his knees until he came to the fly screen and could see the two dozing forms entwined within.

Staring through the screen some memory stirred of the pleasure of holding someone, stroking their golden hair, and a flash of a smile and blue eyes, but then it disappeared in a red hungering instant as he inhaled another lungful of their humid, sweaty forms and a primal moan escaped his lips. This was like the desperate moan of a man building to climax only to have his girlfriend check her watch mid-thrust and tell him she's got to get to the office, as she leaves him with one last lingering squeeze of her pelvic muscles around the tip of his penis.

"Mmmmmh. Honey, you alright?" The one body murmured, a male with his hairy torso bare and a broad forehead, his long blonde hair caught in a pony tail pulled through a leather thong. The other form was entwined in a sleeping bag despite the heat, and an "mmmmh" emerged from a nest of auburn hair next to the man's shoulder. The rest of the tent was a haphazard array of clothes, books and toiletries.

The flavour of their bodies was too much this close, even with the scent of insect repellent adding a slightly acidic taint. He scratched and grabbed at the mesh, trying to press his way through, but the fabric only pressed in a half foot until the material and fly-strings went taught. His body ached with frustration and another long, low moan escaped his lips.

This time the man woke up fully and his blue eyes fastened on the white-bearded, wild-eyed face staring through the fly-screen.

"What the fuck? Are you jerking off to us, you bloody pervert?"

Klaus kept moaning now, and was clawing, biting, straining at the canvas. He couldn't tear through, but one of the corner tent pegs eased out of the ground and part of the tent lurched inward. At the same instant as he fell forward the man's foot shot out and kicked him solidly in the face breaking his nose and sending him toppling backwards towards the fire-pit.

He felt a brief moment of shock, though no real pain, just the old human instincts expecting it to hurt like buggery. The girl's shrill scream was more piercing than the broken nose. His limbs felt sluggish and uncoordinated, and he struggled and squirmed his way to his knees and then back to his feet.

A fist connected with his left cheek and he staggered back

again. But before he could lash out he had a momentary flash of a dark cylinder like antiperspirant in the hands of the girl, before his eyes misted over and he inhaled a lungful of fluoro-carbons and insect repellent. He recoiled, expecting an acid burn, or to be choking, but it was harmless except that the mist covered his eyes and blinded him.

"Grab our wallets and GPS. Then get in the kayak and cast off, babe."

"What about you?"

"Just get in there. I'll be right behind you."

Even blinded he surged in the direction of the man's voice. He received a flurry of further punches to his face and torso, but they bounced off him and Klaus almost succeeded in grappling with him.

"Shit, I think he's trying to bite me."

"I don't know what he is, but he smells feral. Gangrene. Or maybe leprosy. Don't let him touch you!"

Klaus' eyes had started to clear from the spray just as he saw the man hefting one of the oars, and a moment later it was whistling towards his head. Half-stumbling as he lurched forward, Klaus managed to partially duck below it, and was just clipped across the top of his skull. The man was off-balance for a moment as the oar hadn't made the full contact that he'd expected, and whilst he was trying to steady himself, Klaus lumbered forward and bear-hugged him, and they both fell to the ground.

"Get off him you diseased fuck," the woman shouted, but she had already started floating away from the shore. She pulled her legs out of the kayak's belly, and swung them over the side.

And slipped straight to the ground as her feet glided on the slimy rocks. *Fucking blue-green algae.*

Meanwhile Klaus' mouth was slavering, with the hot flesh of the man so close. He hugged him tighter, and brought his mouth down to the crook of the man's neck and bit into the fleshy curve of tendon with a savage snarl.

As the first morsels of flesh hit his taste buds, he was overwhelmed by such ecstasy that he lost grip for a moment. It was enough. In a surge of sharp elbows and knees the man broke free, and scrambled to the water's edge.

For Klaus, the ecstasy turned into sudden clarity. The hunger vanished and he realised with revulsion that he was chewing on human flesh. He saw the depraved, pathetic sight he'd become, scrabbling through brush and dirt as a red-suited cannibal. He also realised that this had happened before, this cycle of hungering insanity followed by the return of his humanity.

"Nooooooo," he cried, spitting the flesh and skin out and dry-retching onto the shore. As he looked up he saw that the woman had an oar raised, and the man had a large rock poised to split on Klaus' skull.

"Wait, please wait... let me tell you who I am."

* * *

"You're going to have to Turn, Klaus, that's the only conclusion that my associates and I can come to."

The two figures were by a fireplace that was burning a pungent mix of reindeer shit and lichen covered twigs, the pitiful little flames taking the edge off the minus thirty odd that locked the land in its winter darkness outside the cabin. One of the individuals was standing.—Karl-Heinz von Thüringen—a tall, well manicured German businessman in jeans and a shirt, accompanied by a corduroy jacket and brown loafers. He didn't carry himself with the fully-suited pretentiousness of the banking crowd, nor with the scruffy disdain of an academic either. He occupied a middle shelf, with an attentive, professional demeanour, who could take himself to a concert, a weekend barbecue, the weekend Football game with the kids, or as was the case today, standing by a fireplace in a cabin in the midst of the frozen northern tundra of Finland opposite Klaus. Saint Klaus.

Klaus also detested pretentiousness, insisting from the beginning of his phone call to <u>Thüringen, Eiben & Associates</u> that Karl-Heinz drop the silly "Saint" nonsense, or any other God-awful bastardisations like "Santa" or "Kris Kringle." Where the hell had anyone conjured that one from anyway? He was berthed in one of the four recliners in a blue Adidas tracksuit. One of the elves—*Rumpel was it?*—had said that the vertical stripes of the sports jacket didn't do anything to flatter his straining waistline, but he was just happy not have to bother with the whole palava of his jolly red suit. If he had his way he'd have a nice clean shave for the first time in a hundred and sixty years, but the elves wouldn't let him near a razor. "Don't destroy the brand." He'd been told by the moody elf Gaudron another time. "You've got to keep true to the image and tradition."

"What do you mean 'Turn'?" Klaus asked.

"Well, even with spending much of your year hibernating in your cryo-tanks here, there's only so long that you can be preserved. And remember for the first hundred odd years that tech wasn't around and the elves were literally putting you on ice. Hibernating like a bear."

"I've done alright so far," Klaus grumbled, his cheeks flushing.

"You saw your last medical," Karl-Heinz continued relentlessly, "Even with your latest liver transplant and a new heart valve there are only so many more root beers and mulled wines, or mince pies and skewers of caribou rare-bit, that your body will take."

"You don't remember the lean times though," he protested.

"Lean times? With all due respect Klaus, your body hasn't seen lean times in many decades, in fact I'd go out on a limb and suggest for at least a century."

"Well you should know. Your firm's been working with me since before The Great War. And you have been working with me for most of those years," he leaned back scratching at his waistline, staring into the fire, "You know what Karl-Heinz, I honestly think it's time I pack it in, and actually let my body rest. Forever. And visit that place in the sky."

"You can't be serious? Where's this coming from? That's not what I'm suggesting at all. Is this the Port speaking?"

"Totally serious. I think it's time."

"Klaus, look me in the eye and tell me that you truly have lost the feeling of joy from making millions of dreams come true."

"Honestly, the letters that arrive at the North Pole these days are just outrageous in their 'requests' and some are downright ungrateful. And to be honest, nobody believes anymore anyway. It's all capitalist shite, and I think that Coca Cola licensing deal you signed for me was the biggest sell out."

"What—"

"Let me read you one, that'll give you some idea of the little ungrateful shits out there," he reached down the side of the recliner to a pile of papers, then planted a pair of small wire-rimmed reading glasses on the end of his nose, coughed once, and recited, "Santa, thanks for the PS1. Unfortunately that was already out of date by like six years. Replace it with a PS3." he finished reciting. "So do you think he'd be impressed if he finds a toy car or a mountain bike under the tree on Christmas Eve? Do you know the pressure I'm under! We've got the most advanced register of births and deaths on the planet..."

"Look, don't take the tone to heart. It doesn't mean they're ungrateful. It's just the way kids talk these days, the world's a lot less respectful of elders than when you or I grew up."

"I—"

"Do you remember the Fischer debacle? When you were laid up that year with a torn Achilles?"

"Yeah, sure. Never trust a bloody American to do a Finn's job..." and he was off on a favourite rant of his that Karl-Heinz had heard dozens of times.

Karl-Heinz sat patiently through the old man's barrage. He could afford to, after all, with the mint in consulting fees this brought his firm's way, a "Change management and resourcing solutions" practice from long before those terms were ever used. He was from the line of great Augsburg bankers that had helped fund and elevate great and notorious families over the centuries.

"Klaus, just listen to me. We need you here. The world needs you here. Do you think we could elevate one of those shopping mall 'Santa' licensees to take this on? Or one of the elves? Rumpel perhaps? Come on, we've got to keep some dignity in this role, and a two foot five 'Santa' ain't going to cut it. What I am offering you is eternal life."

"I've already got that, thanks. The cryo-tanks. And I'm fed up with it, all that glycerol shit being pumped into me before I get frozen, like I'm some car in mid-winter, then waking up in the tanks with tubes in my arms, nose and dick, and weeks of therapy ahead. Do you know how much it hurts to have *that* tube pulled out? And I've that to look forward to every year when I get woken up."

"But that's exactly what I'm suggesting. You can have the eternal life without going through that. Just one bite."

Actually, a series of bites were needed for a full transformation. And Klaus had disappeared too soon.

* * *

Elsewhere. Another fireplace.

The fire wasn't there for warmth. The evening sun was still blistering as Klaus watched a billy-can of water simmering its way to boiling point for a cup of tea. He was sitting across from the camping couple, who'd introduced themselves as "Ben and Erika from Jo-burg". Klaus' eyes darted down to Ben's shoulder every so often, and then glanced away ashamed and apologetic.

They'd taken his attack and breakdown amazingly well, considering they hadn't split his skull open, nor even rung the police. And he could definitely forgive them the fishing wire that they'd used to truss his arms and legs, with just enough length to let him shuffle, or to open his hands to hold a mug, or to prod at his swollen nose and cheek. He would have taken the same precautions if he was in their shoes.

"So you want some kind of miracle, for me to prove that I really am Him?"

"No offence mate, but we did stop believing in Him when we were like in first grade."

"Well I could tell you your address when you were 13, and what presents you got at Christmas that year," Klaus replied.

"So could my stalker."

"Ok, how about this, what if I get Rudolph and his buddies to appear. Or one of my elves."

"Sure. An elf would be a great laugh."

He knew they were just humouring him, a senile old fool who had attacked them, but he felt like surprising them. Sure it would pinpoint him to Karl-Heinz, but he couldn't go on like this. After all he didn't know when the hunger would overpower him again and he was treasuring these precious moments of returned reality and the normality of a cup of tea.

128

Hot tea. Soothing, yet somehow so thin. Flavourless.

I need fresh, hot fluid.

Direct from a vein – crimson, molten, gushing!

He shook his head to clear those thoughts; his stomach's darker cravings were already re-awakening. He closed his eyes, meditating and conjuring up the image of his timber hut, like Mawson's Antarctic outpost, a wind battered, lone survivor on the barren tundra of northern Finland. He then looked into the fire pit before him and talked into the flames, and at the same instant his voice projected through the hearth in his home all those hundreds of kilometres distant.

"Gaudron?"

"Klaus? Where have you been?" The voice that came back was high-pitched and surprisingly chirpy. Gaudron was usually as welcoming as the prospect of pulling on wet socks.

"No time to talk now," he could feel the hunger gnawing at him now, "but can you get Rumpel or one of the other chaps to pull out a sled and get down to me? It's time for me to come home." He realised how this exchange would appear to the Joburg couple: another tick in the *Cuckoo's Nest* checklist for him, talking to a fire as though it was replying. Vanity was irrelevant now though, because he needed Karl-Heinz to fix him somehow, to stop the mindless hunger taking control again.

The harmony of meditation disintegrated as a savage wave of hunger surged through his body, making him shiver with cold fever under the blazing sun. Despite being tied up, he launched himself at the couple with the grace of a sack-race contestant, crouching at the knees and throwing himself bodily through the fire and the still simmering pail of water. The couple tumbled backwards off the log they were sitting on, as he landed in an ungainly heap, one leg in the fire, the water catching him in a steaming deluge. He could smell their skin, so tantalising with its hint of cold, fearful sweat and he squirmed his body pathetically along the ground towards their feet like some lumpy caterpillar.

Ben stamped a foot on his back and grabbed the fishing twine, pulling it tight so that Klaus could barely wriggle.

Erika's eyes were thoughtful. "I don't think he can help himself. Whatever disease he's got, he feels that he needs human flesh and blood. So I'll give him that. At least until we get him to a doctor."

"You are not serious. We should string up the loony and get the hell out of here."

"Don't be a prat," Erika muttered. "We all have days where we just lose it, when we've just broken up with someone and curse the whole friggin' world."

"Yeah, but we don't go and bite people like it's the Night of the Living Dead either!"

Erika kneeled next to Klaus's head and pulled out a knife from their cooking utensils. She pressed the edge against her wrist. "We'll see if a few drops of my blood will keep him from going psycho on us."

"No way in hell. He's already bitten me, so if anyone is going to do this it'll be me."

She ignored Ben's bravado bullshit and pulled the blade across the inside of her wrist, enough for a fine line to appear, and blood soon beaded along the wound. Klaus' face was on its side as he lay prostrate. She held her arm a half foot above his mouth and tried to aim the droplets at his lips, though the first couple splattered into his dirty beard, adding an ochre shade to it. He twisted his face, moaning with need and his tongue flickered to the hairs at the corner of his mouth where the first drops had landed. Erika pushed down on the cut so that more blood eased out and then dripped onto his lips. After his tongue had flickered out for the first half dozen drops, it seemed to take effect and his struggles stopped again.

He pressed his face into the ground and she thought she heard him whisper, "I'm so sorry."

"Let him go Ben, he's with us again."

They heard a crunch of twigs behind them, at the edge of the trees, and a polite cough. "That was very noble of you, giving your blood out of pity like that." The stranger spoke with a north European accent, maybe German or Polish, with the way he interchanged the words "voz" and "werry". They turned to find a handsome man in jeans and a cuff-linked shirt strolling casually from the woods as though they weren't fifty or so kilometers from the nearest town.

"I'm Karl-Heinz, an old acquaintance of Klaus'. Thank goodness you found him. I need to complete the transformation. After all, it's St. Nicholas Day in a few days' time." Karl-

Heinz's eyes and voice were calm and compelling. Ben and Erika moved numbly to the side, as he kneeled next to Klaus and gently lifted his trussed body to cradle him on his knees. He embraced Klaus, his lips brushing the nape of his neck, and Karl-Heinz opened his mouth unnaturally wide. They caught a glimpse of extra-long incisors gleaming in the sun.

TIS' THE SEASON

J. RODIMUS FOWLER

Story Art Cover
By David Naughton-Shires
http://www.TheImageDesigns.com

Dedication
To the ghost who watches me while I sleep...I see you too.

Author Bio
Jason Rodimus Fowler was born in 1976 and hails from Raleigh, North Carolina. He has had a passion for horror and the absurd since he was a small child, which he blames in part on his babysitters, who just happened to have been Monty Python and Rod Serling -via- the Electric God/television. When he was twelve years old or so his mother handed him a copy of Clive Barker's The Damnation Game, and it changed his life forever. J. Rodimus began to write short horror fiction. His twisted tales of fear and retribution range from battling hordes of the undead, to true love among demon fodder.

Tis' The Season

By J. Rodimus Fowler

It's Christmas day and some of the legend, some of what you know, is true. Santa Claus did come and Rudolph did lead the 'Sleigh', except he led it straight to an abandoned church just outside of Little Rock, Arkansas. Rudolph was no reindeer though, he was...infected. He was a vampire. Our story begins now, Christmas day, sunrise.

* * *

Kristoff Van Kringle stared down at the pile of ash and bone with no remorse, his mind fueled by rage and hatred now. There was once a time when he and Rudolph were friends, but now Rudolph was just the means to an end, just bait. Kristoff had captured Rudolph and released him just before sunrise, knowing that the vampire would immediately seek the refuge of his sanctuary, the safety of his master. He followed his former friend to St. Luke's, but there wasn't enough time for Rudolph to get inside before the first rays of the sun took him. In the end he had done his job, Black Peter was just inside the church.

Van Kringle felt the warmth of the morning sun upon his back and the spark of warmth from the burning vampire at his feet and raised his head high to take a deep breath, he so loved the smell of sulfur in the morning. The wind picked up and scattered the charred remains of Rudolph across his red leather boots, further fueling his hatred for the vampire filth. He glanced down at the ash, snarled and stomped what was left of the skull, crushing it under his heel.

Kristoff walked over to his massive pick-up truck, which had the word 'Sleigh' painted across its crimson sides, and began to prepare for work. The 'Sleigh' had a set of silver deer antlers for a hood ornament and dark tinted windows. Something inside the cab of the truck was growling and raising Hell, it was making the whole vehicle shake.

Kristoff calmly walked past the doors, never even glancing up at them, and opened the toolbox in the bed of the truck. He inserted short oak stakes into the grooves on each side of his boots and into the slots on the lower legs of his black leather pants. He strapped on a lightly armored Kevlar vest and a pair of armored gloves to match. His belt had a sheath on each side that housed a pair of twin Roman war hammers. They were made of pure silver and about twenty four inches in length with a sharp eight inch spike on one end and a small blunt head on the other. He covered it all with a long red trench coat that drooped down over the top of his boots. His long hair partially covered his face and his long grey beard hid the crucifix that rested around his neck.

The sun was shining bright and Kristoff was suited up, so it was time to deliver some gifts. He grabbed a large burlap sack, threw it over his shoulder and made his way to the front of the abandoned church that Rudolph had led him to. Black Peter is what Kristoff named the creature that had killed so many of his friends and Black Peter had been very, very naughty.

There was a routine that Kristoff liked to follow when he invaded a nest, but he was driven by a shrewd personal hatred now and he wasn't thinking rationally. This was the closest he'd ever been to Black Peter with the sun on his side and he wasn't going to let him slip away this time.

He placed the sack on the bottom step, reached inside and pulled out a whole case of beer bottles and sat them on the step beside the bag. He began to throw the gasoline filled bottles right through the stained glass windows of the church and the gas began to spread.

He threw the last bottle and reached inside his coat pocket to retrieve a short stubby cigar and a pack of matches. After lighting his stogie and taking a few puffs, he grabbed a single stick of dynamite from the sack and ignited the fuse with the cherry of the cigar.

Kristoff smiled wide as the dynamite spun end over end through the air. The fuse made a sharp cracking sound as it burned faster from the whirling wind. Then it exploded against the front door, destroying it completely and taking a large portion of the exterior wall down with it. The gas caught fire and spread like a river of flame across the chapel. The sun also smiled wide, it shined into the new entrance like a guiding light from Heaven above.

Kristoff threw the burning butt of the cigar into the bag and lashed it shut tight. Then he threw the whole bag into the middle of the church and stepped to cover, away from the opening. When the sack exploded it shook the ground outside almost as much as it did inside, making Kristoff fall to one knee. Dark red flames licked at the walls inside of the church and jutted out of the broken windows. Van Kringle felt the heat across his brow and took a deep breath once again.

Suddenly two men were standing between him and his truck. Ghouls, not men, forced to work for their undead masters, to do their daylight bidding. They fed on vampire blood so they were stronger than men but their flesh was just as weak. The truck began to rock from side to side, whatever was inside was furious.

Kristoff quickly grabbed both of his hammers, so fast that the hammers could have been magnetized to his hands. He charged the ghouls, running at full sprint until the last second, in which he ducked low and shoulder blocked the ghoul on the left. Kristoff hit the ghoul with full momentum sending both, he and it, crashing to the ground. He ended up on top of the ghoul and quickly slammed a hammer down into the side of the ghoul's face, crushing its eye socket and dislocating its jaw. He went to strike it again, but the other ghoul grabbed his arm and pulled him over backwards. Kristoff dropped one of his hammers in the struggle, but he replaced it with one of the stakes from his boot.

The ghoul was blindly striking at his body, which was sufficiently protected. When Kristoff saw his chance, he drove the short wooden stake into the ghoul's leg, just above the knee. The ghoul winced back in pain and was quickly met with a hammer spike to the top of the head. It dropped to the earth instantly with a stake in its leg and a hole in its head. Kristoff walked over to the hammer-smashed ghoul, who was still twitching on the ground, raised his boot and stomped its head with a sharp twist of the heel. The twitching stopped.

The flames had burned off the initial gasoline and most of the large fires had settled down. He wasn't trying for a structural fire, he knew how to do that as well, but with that kind of damage it would only trap the vampire until the cover of night, where it would dig itself out and flee. Kristoff had only wanted to startle the nest, to let the sun shine inside and to let his presence be known. As long as the sun was on his side the vampire had nowhere to run. It was inside the church, in the darkness, waiting, for it now knew it would have to fight to live.

Kristoff mumbled aloud as he gathered his breath along with his other hammer, "I'm getting too old for this shit." He was only forty two, but they had been forty two long, hard years.

The *old man*, with hammer and stake at the ready, entered the church, but stayed in the sunlight. He looked around and paused while his eyes adjusted. He heard hissing sounds from all around him and saw shadows moving inside of shadows by the altar of the church. Underlings, the weakest of vampires, the newly turned, there were at least three or more scurrying around. Kristoff returned his hammer to its sheath and dropped down to one knee. He placed a stake on the floor in front of him touching the edge of the shade.

He was almost close enough for the creatures to reach him, but he never looked up. Two of the underlings crept along the floor sniffing and hissing, trying to understand what the man in the red coat was doing. When they were so close he could smell their breath, he pulled a small mirror from the sleeve of his coat and sent a reflection of sunlight across the room in front of him in a horizontal motion. The beam of light was like a laser to the vampires and cut them both clean in half, cauterizing the wounds along the way. The light struck one vampire across the heart killing it instantly, but it cut the other one across the lower abdomen, it still had use of its arms and howled aloud as it tried to scamper off. Kristoff grabbed the stake from the floor and leapt on top off the vampire, striking it with a single killing blow.

Kristoff, who was now fully engulfed in darkness, reached for his hammers, but the remaining underlings rushed him from three different directions, there had been five of them hiding in the darkness instead of three. He was fast enough to grab one hammer, but the closest vampire snatched his other arm before he had a good grip. Kristoff spun around, as fast as lightning striking, and smashed the vamp that had him by the arm. The underling fell to the floor.

Kristoff's hammer got lodged in the wound and fell to the

floor along with the vampire's corpse. Before he could react he was grabbed from both sides and put in a death grip. They had both of his arms pinned by his sides, but their heads were so low they couldn't reach any of his flesh to sink their teeth into. The Kevlar vest was worth its weight.

The vampires couldn't let go to re-grip because they weren't strong enough to hold off the man individually. Kristoff reached out with his armored gloves and gripped the underlings where ever his hands found flesh. He pushed and pulled with all of his might and forced himself and the two vampires into the sunlight a few feet from where they struggled. The underling's bodies rapidly burned into two piles of ash and bone, covering the toes of Kristoff's boots. He looked down at the mess and snarled again.

The hardwood floor at the altar came splintering up in a thunderous blast, a vampire emerged from the hole in the floor. It was Donner, another former friend of Kristoff's and he was strong, he'd been turned for almost a year. Donner winked at Kristoff, swung his clawed hands at the air in front of him and let out an ear-piercing roar.

Kristoff stood his ground in the sunlight, reached inside his jacket pocket and pulled out another stogie. A few minutes later Kristoff was blowing smoke rings at Donner, who was pacing back and forth, and roaring and grunting. The Vampire was getting impatient.

Kristoff pitched the butt of the cigar against the vampire's chest and said, "Alright Donner, you damned reptile, let's get this over with!"

Donner showed his fangs and began to swat at the air and roar even louder. Kristoff gripped his remaining hammer tight and readied himself. The time for action was now. He stepped into the shade and Donner struck at him immediately. He ducked the vampire's claws and rolled across the floor behind it and dropped into the hole in the floor.

His eyes were adjusted now, but he saw nothing and everything around him was quiet, which was a bad sign. Where was Black Peter? Donner dropped into the hole, landing right in front of Kristoff, who was ready. He swung the hammer as hard as he could into Donner's chest. The eight inch silver spike pierced the vampire's heart and stuck all the way through the creature, leaving its shiny tip protruding out of its back.

Kristoff searched every inch of the church, but there were no more vampires inside. He spent hours tearing holes in the walls in search of hiding places and crawling through the muck underneath the church.

When he finally returned to the yard out front, the sun was about to set. He looked over at his rocking *'Sleigh'*, the thing inside was going crazy. Then it happened the last rays of the sun disappeared.

A loud wicked laughter echoed out through the night sky. Kristoff gripped both of his hammers and looked around every direction. His eyes rested on an old well not too far from where his truck was parked. Before he could move, a black shadow, faster than his eyes could even see, flew out of the well and ripped one of the hammers from his hand. In another black flash, the other hammer was gone as well. Kristoff reached for a stake but something hit him in the chest sending him crashing to the ground. As soon as he regained his footing the vampire hit him again, knocking him back down.

Kristoff, with bloodied lips, sat up on one knee with his eyes fixed on the ground, pulled out a stake and placed it on the soil in front of him and said in a calmly manner, "Hey you, Black Peter, I've got something a little something for you." Then he reached into a small pocket on the sleeve of his coat and retrieved something, never looking up.

The master vampire showed no fear and moved in closer to Kristoff. He spoke confidently, "Your mirror tricks won't work without the sun Mr. Kringle." Then he started up with the wicked laughter again.

Kristoff held up a little piece of black plastic with a few little buttons on it. Black Peter never stopped laughing. The man looked up at the vampire and smiled then he pressed one of the buttons as he screamed aloud, "Come Blitzen! Come Comet!"

The tinted windows of the *'Sleigh'* rolled down and two large hounds with glowing red eyes came bolting out like two dark flashes in the night. In less than a second, they had Black Peter on the ground and were ripping his flesh to shreds. He tried to fight back, but the Hell hounds were relentless. Blitzen ripped his entrails out while Comet fed on the flesh from the vampire's throat. Just before the spark had completely faded away from Black Peter's eyes Kristoff leaned in close to the vampire and said, "Funny thing about feeding my dogs here vampire meat, it makes them real strong, and it makes them real hungry!"

Story Art Cover
By David Naughton-Shires
http://www.TheImageDesigns.com

Dedication

To Tell, because you're a Vampire lover.
Even if this one doesn't sparkle!

Author Bio

Emma Ennis comes from Ireland, but has been living in Norway for two years. Though she had attempted a brief stint at writing back in her younger days, it was only in November of last year that she got back into it and started to get published. Since then she has had almost thirty short stories published or accepted for publishing in various anthologies in US and UK. October of this year will see the release of her first, solo collection of short stories to be entitled 'Red Wine and Words,' achieving a lifelong dream.

Yuletide Gathering
By Emma Ennis

In the dead of night there came a knock on the door. Despite the lateness of the hour, the two inhabitants were still up, pacing the floors. When they heard the sound they looked at each other, hope gleaming in their tear stained eyes. Could it be?

Without another second's delay, the man strode to the door and flung it open. A stranger stepped over the threshold and closed the door swiftly behind him. The weak light of the candle fell upon his face and the woman gasped. If it had not been for the wiggling bundle he held in his arms, she would have run screaming from the room.

"You have been given another chance," said the stranger. His voice, though melodic, carried with it a chill from beyond the grave. "But things are going to be different, and it comes with a price."

At that precise moment, his cargo gave an extra strenuous kick, and a fold of its coverings fell away, revealing a tiny arm that terminated in five pudgy fingers. On the shoulder was a raspberry coloured birthmark in the shape of a heart. The man and woman looked at each other, an unspoken agreement passing between their interlocked eyes.

"We're listening," the man said.

* * *

Malachi leaned against the stone casement, gazing down at the townsfolk as they scurried around the village at the foot of the hill; his hill. There would have been something close to frenzy in the way they hurried to and fro, if it hadn't been for that damnable cheer that leaked from them all like a pungent discharge. They called to each other in the street, hugged and kissed, faces all aglow. If he were capable of it, he would have vomited.

It was the same every year. They were preparing for Christmas.

And what a ridiculous tradition that was too. Stupid, brainwashed sheep – they did not even realize what they were celebrating. They believed themselves so pious to be observing the anniversary of the birth of their Lord and Savior, when what they were really rejoicing over would blanch their happy, rosy little cheeks if they knew.

It was many years ago, hundreds, but Malachi could well remember the *real* celebrations – a glorious week of unadulterated lawlessness in the pagan calendar. In that week nobody could be punished for their crimes, whether against people or property, and no matter how heinous. Intoxication, rape – it all went unchecked. And each year, one innocent was selected, fattened and on December twenty-fifth, was sacrificed to end the festival. Allowing the pagans to continue to celebrate that week of debauchery was part of the conversion deal. Then they dubbed the concluding day as the birthday of their king, and lo and behold, a race was Christianized.

So every year these people celebrated the killing of an innocent, while he, Malachi, had to hide. Dumb Christians, dumb humans. Even the trees they hacked down, lugged inside and decorated to the point that the whole of nature cringed in embarrassment – that was another custom left over from their pagan days of worship. It never ceased to amaze him how fickle human beings were. It made his blood boil.

Malachi smiled at the pun and drained his goblet. As maddening as their stupidity was, it was nonetheless his gain. They made things easy for him.

He heard his underling, Byron, come into the room. Malachi had made him a long time ago then let him loose, allowing him some time to adjust – a sort of training period as it were – but he had summoned him back four years ago to serve him. Now his presence reminded Malachi that his glass was empty.

"I'm thirsty," he observed. "Enough of this farce."

He flung the cup to the ground, sending Byron scurrying after it.

"Let us make this a Christmas they will remember, and for reasons very real."

"As you wish master."

Malachi turned back to the window. The weak sun had slipped below the horizon and the shadows of darkness slid across the land, swallowing everything in their path. The townsfolk seemed unaware of the demise of day. They usually didn't stay out after dark; there were rumors, legends. People went missing, and turned up again as corpses with strange wounds, their bodies inexplicably emptied of lifeblood. They said a demon lived in the old castle on the hill, a fiend who drank the blood of the innocent.

But at Christmas their caution slipped. Maybe the twinkling lights gave them courage, or the list of gifts they memorized made them forgetful of all else. Whatever the reason, they would pay for their stupidity. Malachi would see to that.

He stood out on the window ledge. Darkness enfolded him and he blended with it, moving as the shadows moved – silent and slinking. He swooped to the ledge below and leapt across to the next, covering an impossible distance. Free falling to the foot of his castle, he moved down the hillside and took refuge in the rooftops of the town. He was fluid, like liquid shadow. His feet made no sound on the roofs or chimneys as he bounded between them with inhuman agility and coordination.

When he was in that mode his eyesight adapted. It was as though time slowed down for him to take in, in intricate detail, his surroundings. His vision homed in, selecting, rejecting. Too old, too open, too controversial... until he found her.

She walked at the edge of the town, where the light of the lanterns did not reach. She was alone, carrying a lush wreath for her door. He watched her from above, following her until he was sure she was the one. Then he overtook her and landed in an alleyway a few paces ahead.

His heightened hearing caught the sound of her soft footfalls approaching and he stepped out into her path. She gasped and stopped. She couldn't see much of him yet, but he could see her. And boy, was she a beauty. Lillith. He read her name on her.

"I apologies if I startled you ma'am." His voice, his words, were music. They surrounded her, filled her head so that nothing else existed.

"It is my own fault. I am foolish to be out so late," she replied. There was relief and the hint of a smile in her tone.

Malachi spread a smile of his own, and stepped closer so she could see him. "That you are Lillith," he agreed.

Her hands lost the wreath she was carrying, and it dropped to the cobbles with a rustle. Her closing throat strangled her scream, but he heard it.

It was his eyes. They always had that effect at first. Right about now he figured they would be glowing red with thirst, pulsating with lust for the tall, slim glass in front of him. They would turn black once he had fed. There was nothing normal about his eyes, not an ounce of human in them.

Her creamy bosom heaved and she started to back away. It could have been the teeth either. Shiny, elongated, sharp – ready to puncture her delicate throat. The woman had heard the superstitions of the town and he could see it in her eyes as she started to believe them. She hadn't up until that very moment, silly, fickle human.

Her fear was a perfume that drove him wild with lust. An almost orgasmic shiver caressed his insides. He would take his time with this one, bring her back to the castle to enjoy her rather than finish her off in the street. It would be his Christmas present to himself.

He smiled, displaying the true length and destructiveness of his canines. A lone tear slid down her cheek. He tasted its salt on the night air, and licked his lips. The superstitions are a little too close to home now, aren't they little Lillith?

She wouldn't fight him. They rarely did. He had that power. He raised his hand and beckoned to her. She came, a little woodenly at first as her brain tried to fight his pull. He brought her right to him, and his eyes travelled down the curve of her neck to the bodice of her gown. He gripped her breast and squeezed. Her back arched to his touch and he bent to kiss her. Oh, he was feeling it now – that Christmas spirit.

His teeth cut her bottom lip and she moaned in pain. A droplet of blood landed on his tongue and it tasted like heaven should. He could have snapped her spine and ate her all up in that split second, but she was too fine a specimen to rush.

Malachi walked her into the alley, then he held her against him and shimmied up onto the rooftops. Her body was soft and warm against his, her breath hot and terrified on his ear. Those things he lacked turned him on the most – a beating heart and rushing veins, body heat, breathing. He was more than ready for her by the time they arrived at the castle.

Taking her upstairs, he threw her onto the bed. He never used it for sleeping, but Byron kept it ready just for such an occasion, the ligatures on the bedposts too. They weren't necessary; ligatures or not, they could not resist him, but he loved the helpless feeling they gave his victims. It made their blood thicker, more potent, like a full bodied wine. Of course, if the longing was on him, he could drop the charm, and let them struggle and fight against the restraints so that it almost felt like a challenge. It all depended on the mood.

Lillith was no different; she felt the fear just as much as all the others. Malachi fucked and drank to almost equal measure. When one desire was momentarily satisfied, he turned to the other. He drained her from her neck, her wrist, her breasts, her inner thighs; so juicy and warm. By dawn she was almost empty and he had to force himself to stop. He could have gorged himself well into the lethal sunrise, but he did not want to empty this bottle all in one night.

So he kept her, and used her again the following night. And the night after that. She was in a lot of pain, but his bite had an anesthetic that dulled it for a short time, so she must have longed for his visits as well as feared them. It was during his absence, in the daylight hours, when she would have craved death the most.

He kept Lillith, but he also took others. He had, after all, promised the town a Christmas to remember. He took the youngest, the favorites, the ones who would be missed the most – the ones who would leave the biggest hole in the joyous Christmas hearts.

He found a young mother and her son. What they were doing out at night he would never know, but they were not for him to worry about; they were for him to take. Night time was his time, and they had wandered onto his patch. He would enjoy watching from the castle as the husband and father went crazy with worry. Christmas would never be the same for him again.

Malachi let the woman, Celeste, watch while he drained the boy. He had mixed emotions about drinking from children. Their blood was so fresh, so pure, it sent his body into drug-like spasms. But they emptied so fast that it was not always worth the hunt. They were more of an expensive appetizer to the main meal as it were.

Speaking of which, he tossed the boy's limp body aside. His

little arm flopped out and landed on his mothers foot. Her bottom lip shook and big tears dropped from her lashes. Malachi took her, sobbing, to the room where Lillith waited, shackled and suffering. At the foot of the bed, he undressed the woman until she was all naked and shivering before him. His hand must have felt like ice against the back of her neck, as he pulled her towards him.

From the bed Lillith whimpered and he smiled, exposing teeth that were as hard and ready as his cock. He drank the woman in front of Lillith's pained eyes, so that she could dream of the relief his venom would give, drive her wild with longing for him.

After the boy, the woman's blood was poor; she was too fond of the port. He threw her away in disgust.

"Byron," he barked, never taking eyes off the struggling victim tied to the bed, "clean up."

His servant slipped from the shadows and bundled the woman into his arms, flinging her over his shoulder like the empty sack she was.

"There is another in the dining room."

Malachi approached the bed. Lillith quit her exertions; she knew by the look on his face that he was coming for her. Her lips formed a single, silent word: 'Please.'

Stupid girl, be careful what you wish for. He could withhold the anesthetic too. Tonight he would not give it to her. He would let her feel every puncture, every thrust. Maybe that would teach her to be so presumptuous.

* * *

Byron lugged the two bodies down into the bowels of the castle. There was an old well to the sewer there, he could weight the bodies and dump them in. He dropped them by the pit and flung the wooden cover aside. The stench of decay and feces hit him in the face like a wave and he stepped back in disgust. The smell attracted a team of rats, and one of them scurried right by his foot. They underestimated him, thinking he was just another human, and hence did not foresee the swiftness of his foot. He sent one of them flying through the air with a startled squeak. Its body hit the opposite wall with a thud, and it scurried no more.

The walls were crumbling and he gathered up some of the debris and shoved it into the clothing of the corpses. Before he tossed the boy in, he bent and sank his teeth into his tiny wrist. He took a long draught, then winced and spit it out. Dead blood. He rolled the body into the sewer and turned to the lady.

He was sick of being the undertaker, sick of leftovers. Before, he had been free. He had romanced the blood out of whomever he so desired, mostly ladies like the one his *master* kept. He would have liked some time with her.

He bit into the woman's wrist and was surprised to feel some warmth tickle the nerve endings of his teeth. Her eyelids fluttered. There was life in this one yet – he could taste the spark. He began to drink. It wasn't an exquisite bouquet, or expensive, but it was blood, however little of it Malachi had left in her.

A sudden thought formed in his head and he stopped guzzling. The idea sparked a light behind his eyes. He looked at the woman, and changed the course of his teeth.

* * *

It became something of a game for Malachi, to tease Lillith with his victims. Sometimes he walked away afterwards, leaving her crying and pleading for him. Other times he would help himself to some of her too, but as he approached nowadays, there was always a new fear in her eyes, the fear that he would not deliver the drug she so badly craved.

Malachi played around with the thought of changing her; she would make a beautiful vampire. But not yet. There was still some blood in those veins, still some residual heat between her legs that he could enjoy before he made her eternally cold.

Each night he stood at the window in the tower to watch the commotion in the town as they made frantic searches for their loved ones. He had to admit though, he had thought there would have been more pandemonium, that Christmas would have been forgotten, but they were still making their ridiculous preparations. They had even erected a giant tree in the centre of the village.

151

He would just have to work harder, hone his choices. He took more and more. He had so many victims that he didn't have the time, or the capacity to drain them all fully, and most nights Byron carted armfuls of half empty bodies down to the sewers.

Two nights before Christmas, Malachi bagged his greatest gift – a newborn baby. Babies, to vampires, were like sushi to humans; the cream of the crop. He heard the mother's cries deep into the night. It was music to his ears. He imagined the things they had squandered their money on – toys decorations, clothes – all forgotten now. Their foolishness, their greed, it was all for nothing. If they had spent more time watching their son, they would have something to celebrate. He had probably done the kid a favor.

The tears stopped somewhere just before daybreak, when Malachi was underground, buzzing off the blood of the newborn. He cursed the sun and the dawn of day because he longed to watch the town mourn the loss of the infant.

But the next night, when he arose to savor the fruits of his harvest, he was met with an atmosphere of celebration and expectation in the town. The inhabitants milled around the village tree. Their merry laughter tinkled on the cool air, reaching him in the tower. Strains of music and singing came from a band of carolers under the church lantern. Children ran in rings around the legs of the adults, dressed in their finest.

The song ended and everyone fell silent, turning to the tree. Four figures approached it. With practiced movements, they set light to the candles decorating the tree. When it was all lit up, they stood back and the whole village joined together in joyous song.

Malachi stepped back from the window, his eyes wide, his nostrils flaring.

"Why aren't they mourning?" he roared. "What is *wrong* with these people? They insist on celebrating, even as their numbers are thinned?"

Rage overtook him. He stormed through the castle, ripping doors from their hinges and tossing them aside as if they were paper. Were they so primitive that they had no emotions? How dare they ignore him and what he had done.

His blind anger took him to Lillith's room. She was weak

and didn't struggle so much anymore those days. He slapped her, hard, and she moaned, but barely moved. He wanted her to move, he wanted her to fight. He bit into her jugular, holding back the sedative. She moaned louder and he dug in deeper, burying his teeth in her bloodstream. But still her body lay limp. He tore off his clothes and climbed on top of her. She lay there and took it, and Malachi roared in frustration, hitting her again and again. The bitch wanted to die? So be it.

He took up her arm and ripped open a hole in her wrist, exposing the veins. The flow of blood was sluggish and he sucked hard until he heard her last exhale. So much for changing her. But there would be others. Right now there was insolence that needed to be dealt with.

He swooped out the window and down into the town. Not one family did he leave immune; he took at least one from each. It was almost dawn when he quit his spree, but he was pleased with himself. The next day, Christmas day, they would awake to find their town desiccated. See the fools rejoice then.

Malachi rested uneasy; he had engorged himself to an un-comfortable extent, and on top of that he was eager to see the reaction to his nights work. It took forever for the darkness to come, but eventually it did. As he climbed the stairs to the tower, he lamented the loss of Lillith. It would have been nice to sink into her, in more ways than one, after watching the devastation.

There was nobody to be seen in the town, and Malachi grinned in triumph. There were lights shining behind most of the windows. He could make out the shapes of people inside. He peered closer and strained his ears, trying to see and hear the grief.

His brow furrowed. Through one of the lighted windows he saw a ring of faces, seated around a table. He could not discern their exact conversation, but it sounded like *chatter.*

His head whipped around, scanning all the homes. They were all the same. In one house on the outskirts he could even make out smiles on the faces of the occupants.

The fury rose in him again. He'd had enough of that town. He would kill them all and be done with it. He would end their stupidity tonight.

He found his first victim in the square, standing gazing at

the lighted tree. He landed behind her silently, and inched towards her.

"It's missing something," he stated, his mouth stretching in a menacing grin.

"I agree," the woman replied, and turned.

Malachi's eyes almost popped out of his skull. Before him stood Lillith, her skin as perfect and as pale as alabaster. Her dark hair fell in shiny chocolate waves to her elbows. Her eyes were dark in her pale face, and they bore into him so hard that he was forced to take a step backwards.

From behind the tree, another woman emerged. The candlelight shone on her face and he recognized her. Celeste. A couple stepped from the shadows on the edge of the square, holding a newborn baby. A boy, the village priest, two school girls – all of them gathered in the square before him. He recognized them all.

"You..." he stammered. "I killed you people."

Malachi's eyes widened further when Byron, his scion, stepped up beside Lillith, and she took his hand.

"Not completely," Byron said, to Lillith's delight. She smiled, displaying a glistening set of canines, not yet as long as Malachi's, but longer than normal nonetheless. "You're getting sloppy *master.* I changed them all, down in the sewer."

The crowd of new reborn were gathering around Malachi, closing in on him.

"You want to give us a Christmas to remember?" Lillith asked. She really did make a beautiful vampire. "That's very kind of you."

She inclined her head and Malachi felt strong hands grip him. They dragged his forward, closer to the tree.

"We can celebrate your demise, and the birth of the town, each year, on the twenty-fifth."

They hauled him past her and hoisted him up, lashing him onto the tree. He wasn't worried; as soon as their backs were turned he could easily break the bonds.

But they had foreseen this. Byron stepped up to him. Steel glinted in the candlelight. He drove the blade into Malachi's stomach. Black blood leaked from the opening. Byron sliced his wrists and throat, bleeding him out like a pig. He would not die, but he would be too weakened to struggle.

Lillith approached the tree, a theatrical frown creasing her marble brow.

"Something is off," she mused, tweaking a candle so that the flame licked at Malachi's shirt. He could feel the heat of it, made all the more intense by his own coldness. His hair caught fire and he felt the skin begin to melt and slide from his face.

They all stepped back, forming a semi-circle as the flames engulfed him, spreading their hot agony all over him. His screams made a rich soprano. Someone struck up a song and they all joined in, singing with jubilation, as they watched a Christmas display like no other.

In The Twilight of Christmas
Craig Chenery
To my wife Tera

Each year at Christmas we do something sweet,
And we invite a guest over for something to eat.
This year my wife knew a man she'd adore,
And invited the fellow who moved in next door.

I was sat on the sofa awaiting the knock,
The slight tapping came at seven o'clock.
I opened the door firmly and let our guest in,
He was tall, pale and sparkled and incredibly thin.

"Thanks Jim" he said as he gave me his coat,
I was certain the bastard was eying my throat.
I pulled my collar up close to my face,
And gave him a very quick tour of our place.

He gave a slight glance at our small Christmas tree,
At the pile of our presents and my big screen TV.
"Jane's in the kitchen", I said with a sigh,
"She's making the custard for her apple pie."

We got to the kitchen and Jane said hello,
Showing less cleavage five minutes ago.
Her eyes opened wide as he stepped through the door,
In three rapid steps he had traversed the floor.

He swept Jane up in a warming embrace,
A look of sheer joy swept over her face.
"Thank you coming" she said with a grin,
"May I offer some wine, some vodka or gin?"

"If you don't mind I'll just take some blood,
Dee Mary to cure my hangover's thud."
My, how they laughed at this terrible pun,
As I wondered if I should be grabbing my gun.

We sat down to eat and they started to chat,
As I hacked at my steak and cut off the fat.
The minutes passed by as they continued to talk,

157

Craig Chenery

And I pushed all my peas around with my fork.

Jane's personal questions came fluent and quick
But I think that his answers made him look like a dick
"Tell me some more about your vampire life
Have you been one for long? Have you taken a wife?"

"Your skin is so pretty and your hair is styled fine"
"Yeah, and I have all my suits made by Calvin Klein"
"I'm so glad you came" she said, not skipping a beat
"Can a vampire eat steak?" "No I never eat meat"

"The site of red blood sends chills down my back,
The metallically taste makes me want to yack.
It's not that I'm squeamish, so don't think that please,
In this day and age, I'm just scared of disease."

I couldn't help laughing at what I'd just heard,
"A vegetarian vampire that sounds quite absurd!"
"Keep it up Jim and I'll make you my first,
It doesn't take much to acquire blood thirst."

I let out a sigh at this thinly veiled threat,
And I wondered how bad this dinner would get.
Jane's eyes lit up as he read sonnets and rhymes,
And he told me to "Shut up" at least four or five times.

As the dinner wore on the closer they got,
And my presence therein was quite soon forgot.
I was losing my patience as I played with my knife,
I couldn't believe he was tempting my wife.

I cleared my throat loudly to halt their embrace,
And saw the mad look wash over Jane's face.
It was time to stop this dead in its tracks,
As I launched a tirade of vampire facts.

"Real vampires don't sparkle and they never grow old,
They party all night, at least so I am told.
You can be killed by a stake with an aim true and just,
And as quickly as that can be turned into dust²

A real vampire would come out only at night,
And rip out my throat in one rapid bite.'

In The Twilight of Christmas

"That offer is tempting" he said with a sneer,
"If you like it dear Jane, I'll make Jim disappear."
I couldn't believe it when Jane said "okay",
And asked if the two could be married someday.
"You will have to be turned so we will never grow old,
I will quickly kill Jim before the turkey gets cold."

The last thing I remember as the vampire moved in,
Was the smell of cologne and his sparkly skin.
It was a rather bad ending to a rather bad night,
And it turned out my vampire facts were not right.

I felt the sharp sting as his teeth pierced my skin,
And the blackness of death was soon setting in.
This was the worst Christmas gift I had got in my life,
A vampire bite and divorce from my wife.

As I lay on the floor and drew my last breath,
I eagerly welcomed the wide arms of death.
But to make matters worse as I looked at my skin,
I could see a slight sparkle start setting in.

A Vampire's "Bite" Before Christmas
Rusty Fischer

'Twas the night before Christmas,
And all through the coven
The air felt as cold
As an Eskimo's oven!

The coffins were open
The vampires milling;
As this was the night
For some *Santa* blood spilling!

The vampire's basement
Looked haunted and dusty;
The floors were quite damp
The walls rather... musty.

The air it was filled
With maximum dread;
As just up the stairs
The vampires fled.

The living room looked
Like a warm greeting card;
As to welcome dear Santa
The vamps had tried hard!

A tree it stood shining
The lights they did glitter;
As the vamps shook their heads
And started to twitter.

It wasn't their nature
To get bright and sparkly;
For vampires preferred
To celebrate... darkly.

If they did have a tree
(Which was rather quite rare)
The vamps lit it sparsely
With black balls and devil's hair.

Rusty Fischer

Their vampire leader
Smiled wider than most;
His hair black as tar
His skin white as toast.

His name it was Chauncey
His legend quite vast;
For even among vampires
He was *quite* the badass.

One vamp asked him, "Chauncey,
"Do you think Santa knows...
Of our plan to attack him
And suck dry his toes?"

Chauncey nodded quite gravely
And said with a sigh,
"This isn't the first time
We've tried to drain the big guy."

Chauncey thought with a smile
Of the last 10 decades;
And how they'd tried to trap Santa
And his trusty elf aides.

For Santa had one thing
The vamps sure did not;
A magical bloodstream
That just would not clot!

If only the vamps
Could tap Santa's vein;
Over all the immortals
Their species would reign!

So every year
On the 25th of December;
Vamps all cross the world
Tried Santa to dismember!

And now hooves were tramping
Up on the vamps' ceiling;
As dread in his veins
Chaunce was suddenly feeling!

A Vampire's "Bite" Before Christmas

For now it was time,
To drain the jolly old elf;
Or bring another year of shame
Upon Chauncey's old self.

He readied the vamps
As he put them in their places;
With fangs sticking out
Of their pancake pale faces.

"I don't know what Santa
Has stuck up his sleeve,"
Chauncey said to his minions
Who could no longer breathe.

"But whatever you do,
Take care of yourselves.
And don't fall into the trap
Set by Santa's bad elves!"

Each vamp had a corner
Each vamp had his space;
As the chimney hole spat up
All over the place!

The first crucifix fell
And scattered the lot;
As the vamps ran away
Before they could rot!

The elves quickly followed
As onto the floor;
They rolled one by one
As more followed more.

They each grabbed a cross
And stood side by side;
As across the floor
They started to stride.

Only Chauncey remained
His vamps having scattered;
He had barely noticed
For nothing else mattered...

Rusty Fischer

Save slaying dear Santa
On this Christmas Eve;
For elves or no elves
Santa just couldn't leave.

They elves they did battle
They put up a fight;
But Chauncey prevailed
On this holiday night.

He slayed them quite soundly
Each pint-sized little elf;
Until he was triumphant
(And quite proud of himself!)

But the war wasn't over
It had only begun;
For Santa brought vengeance
And all kinds of fun!

He landed quite squarely
In the fireplace grate;
And said, "Sorry Chauncey;
It appears I'm too late..."

"... to save my dear elves
From your living dead charm;
But have no fear, Chauncey –
Santa's here to do you harm!"

And old Santa meant it
That lively old elf;
He snuffed and he snorted
In spite of himself!

He ripped off his sleeves
And flexed massive biceps;
Old Chaunce stood his ground
Fangs glistening like forceps.

"I see you've been lifting
Your loyal reindeer.
You're mad if you think
You fill me with fear!"

164

A Vampire's "Bite" Before Christmas

Old Santa did wink
And the rumbling it grew;
As eight giant reindeer
Down the chimney they flew!

The reindeer were vicious
As they gathered around;
And knocked poor old Chauncey
Straight onto the ground.

They stomped as they hungered
For some prime vampire pain;
As poor Chauncey tried fighting
Them off quite in vain.

And as each massive paw print
Seared into his skin;
Chauncey's face fairly burst
In a maniacal grin.

He slashed at their ankles
With his ragged, rough claws;
As each tiny reindeer
Fell straight to its paws!

They scattered and scampered
Away from his wrath;
As straight toward Santa
The vamp set a path!

The fat man was turning
To make his escape;
When Chauncey came at him
And chomped on his nape!

But Santa was lively
Quite spritely and quick;
And poor Chauncey got
No more than a lick!

And onto the rooftop
Old Santa did spring;
As into the night
His voice it did ring.

Rusty Fischer

"On Dancer, On Dasher
Don't care if you're bleeding;
Away from this hellhole
We need to be speeding!"

Old Chauncey was wounded
And felt to one knee;
Landing in front
Of that old Christmas tree.

And there, wrapped up nicely
In ribbons and bows;
Was a sight that warmed Chauncey
Straight down to his toes.

A vial, you see
Filled with gooey red stuff;
A sight that filled Chauncey
Fully of holiday guff!

It was from Santa, you see
A gift straight from the heart;
For it was with one pint of blood
The fat man did part.

He'd given old Chauncey
His fondest gift yet;
A tube of his blood
The freshest he'd get!

His wish had come true
Santa's blood was all his;
He poured it all down
But it started to... fizz?

The vampire did choke
On Santa's gag gift!
Just when his spirits
Had started to lift!

It wasn't elf blood
In that little glass tube;
Old Chaunce had been had;
He felt like... a boob!

A Vampire's "Bite" Before Christmas

It was candy Santa'd left him
Under the tree;
And now the fat man
Did cackle with glee.

"It would be too easy,"
Santa called from his sleigh.
"If I gave you my blood;
Just tossed it away."

And then Santa drove
Quite far out of sight;
As his sleigh disappeared
On this cold Christmas night.

And Chauncey retired
To his coffin downstairs;
For some much needed
Old bloody vampire repairs.

And he thought as he nestled
Quite snug in his coffin;
How next year old Santa
He'd better be offin!

169

171

174

175

178

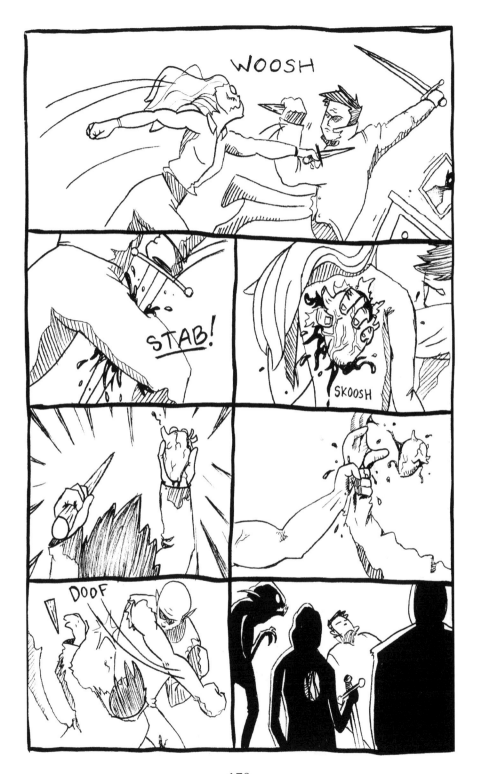

179

180

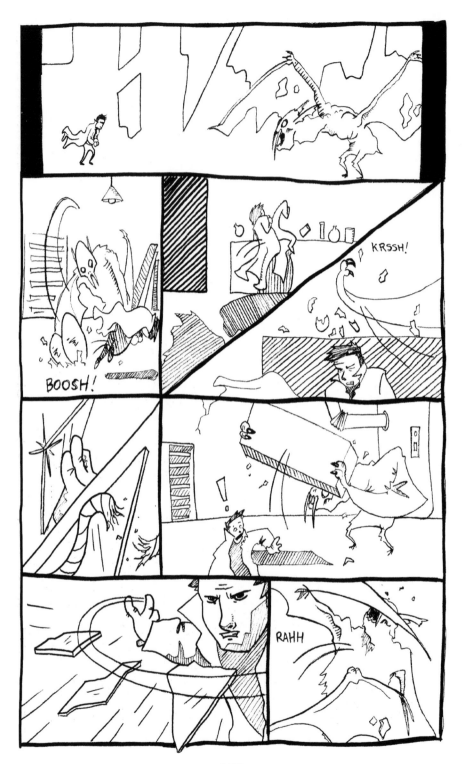

183

185

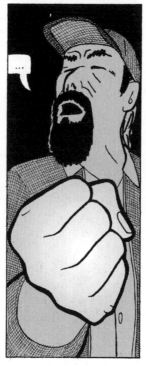

186

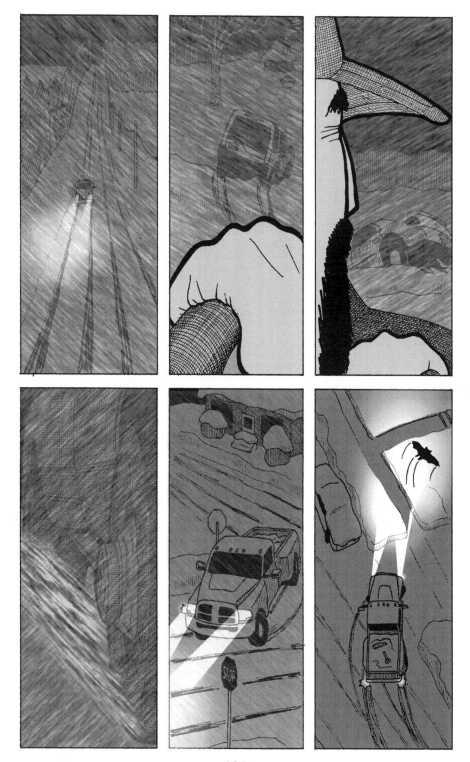

187

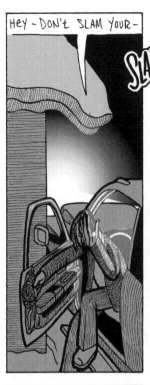

BUT EVEN I REMEMBER CHRISTMAS. I WONDER IF GENEROSITY COULD BE AS NOSTALGIC AS WAGNER.

I DOUBT IT, BUT ONE NEVER KNOWS. MAKE YOUR CASE, BOY.

puh-puh-PLEASE, SIR... I'm... I'm NOT GROWN UP YET. HE'S A CLASS-A DICK, BUT HE'S MY DAD.

I muh-NEED HIM. YOU KNOW, FOR GUIDANCE.

OH, DEARY ME. I MUST SAY I AM MOVED...

...OR I WOULD BE IF I DIDN'T HAVE SUCH AN INTIMATE RELATIONSHIP WITH HUMAN BLOODFLOW. LITTLE **LIAR.**

AND HOW I **LOVE** A GOOD LIE! AHHH-ₐh-ₐh-ₐhhh... I... LAUGH?

NOW **THIS** IS NOSTALGIC. YOU ARE ON MY GOOD SIDE THIS FINE EVE. LET US CONSIDER.

YOU CLAIM TO DESIRE A... A MENTOR? YES - 'MENTOR' IS APT.

WE VAMPIRES SUBSCRIBE WHOLLY TO MENTORING, NECESSARY AS IT IS WHEN CONVERTING PREY TO PREDATOR.

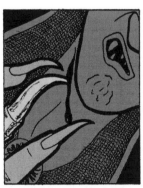

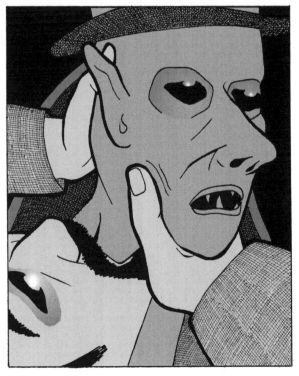

192

193

195

196

MODELS : SHI McCRAY & MICHELLE MORELOS

197

About the Contributors

Craig W. Chenery (Poem Author) is the author of the upcoming book "Blood Splatter: A Guide to Cinematic Zombie Violence, Gore and Special Effects". He has been a fan of the horror genre for most of his life, in particular the zombie genre and is well versed in both cinematic and literary zombie history. He currently resides in Avondale, Arizona with his wife Tera and their daughter Lily.

Rusty Fischer (Poem Author) is the author of several YA supernatural novels, including *Zombies Don't Cry, Ushers, Inc., Vamplayers, I Heart Zombie* and *Panty Raid @ Zombie High.* Visit his blog, www.zombiesdontblog.blogspot.com, for news, reviews, cover leaks, writing and publishing advice, book excerpts and more!

David Naught-Shires (Cover Artist) is an artist and author born in England but now living in Ireland he has written many short stories and create numerous book covers, illustrations and other forms of design, you can learn more about David by visiting one of his many online locations.
www.theimagedesigns.com, www.knightwatchpress.info.
www.facebook.com/theimagedesigns, www.facebook.com/KWP ress This is his second year helping with the Christmas Charity project and hopes to continue into the next year.

Ian Kobe (Cover Artist) was raised by gypsies, and later by the pack of wild dogs that devoured them. Ian lives in Phoenix, Arizona where he spends much of his time daydreaming of fox ownership. He celebrates the entire catalog of Burt Reynolds' films and wishes the ascot would become fashionable again. You can his detritus at squidsicle.com

Rachel Dukes (Cover Artist) Born three months premature, Rachel has always been determined and stubborn. In the first grade, she drew her first comic strips and proclaimed to her teacher that she would like to do comics when she grew up. Rachel has interned at Top Cow Entertainment, was one of the first recipients of the Women Webcomikers Grant NAN, and received her Bachelors of Science in Media Arts and Animation. She currently lives in White River Junction with her husband, Mike, and their cat, Frankie, where she self publishes comics and comic anthologies. She is currently studying for her Masters of Fine Arts at The Center for Cartoon Studies.

Nate Call (Comic Author and Illustrator) is a 25 year old guy living in Orem, Utah with his gorgeous and talented wife, Camie. He is currently going to Utah Valley University majoring in Visual Art and Communication with an emphasis in illustrations. When he's not drawing comics about zombies, he's killing them. In real life. Fueled by his passion for drawing and his hatred for Nazis, Nate looks forward to illustrating his way into the hearts of people everywhere.

Wm Brian MacLean (Comic Author and Illustrator) plays cultural critic in his editorial webcomic, OpinioNation. His other webcomic, Anx, sees many of his forays into storytelling. Anx will likely be the initial venue for an upcoming, serialized autobiography. Find these & other print & online comics at roostertree.com & wbmaclean.com

Lyndal Ferguson (Comic Author and Illustrator), of Beckley, WV, is an artist and a writer. He does CD covers, t-shirt designs, show posters and has had art and stories internationally published in numerous magazines , including ROCK-N-ROLL COMICS, GIRLS AND CORPSES MAGAZINE, HEAVY METAL, OUI, RIP, MR. MONSTER, MONSTER INTERNATIONAL, BLACK CAT 13 and his own comic, DR. BANG. He is currently working on the NURSE HATCHET comic, co-starring CHAINSAW SALLY. He can be reached at lyndalferguson@hotmail.com

About the Editors

Lyle Perez-Tinics (Writer/Editor/Publisher) is the creator of http://www.UndeadintheHead.com a website dedicated to zombie books and the authors. He is the owner & Editor-in-Chief of Rainstorm Press (www.RainstormPress.com) and The Mad Formatter (www.TheMadFormatter.com) a book interior design business. He has stories in many anthologies and is currently working on two novels, *Existing Dead* and *Rising from the Tempest*. He is the mastermind behind *The Undead That Saved Christmas* charity anthology series. He also writes middle grade chapter books under his pen name, Benny Alano.

www.BennyAlano.com

Twitter - @LylePerez @RainstormPress @UndeadintheHead

@Benny Alano

www.Facebook.com/RainstormPress

www.Facebook.com/UndeadintheHead

Joe Filippone is currently a full time actor and writer living in Hollywood California who has always loved vampires. His short stories have appeared in close to forty anthologies including *The Undead That Saved Christmas, Letters From The Dead, Baconology* and numerous others. He is also the author of the YA novel *Real Boys Kiss Boys* and the Christmas novella *The Christmas Cottage*.

coming soon from

KnightWatch Press

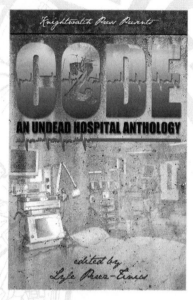

Mark Bliss has spent most of his adult life working at a pawnshop. For years, he has ripped people off with no remorse. That is until the day an elderly woman named Maggie Bliss, walks in through the door and brings an army of living dead with her. DEMENT is a story that truly lives up to its title. Join Mark as he slowly goes insane on the roof of a pawnshop, while the bodies of the dead linger below.

We all know many of the best Zombie flicks and books make their start in or around a hospital but they soon leave the confines of the medical building and start to lay waste to the world but what happens in those first few hours.
" CODE Z - An Undead Hospital Anthology " is a horror anthology with an undead theme. Tales of life excitement and of course the undead. Each story is unique and new.

www.knightwatchpress.info

Printed in Great Britain
by Amazon.co.uk, Ltd.,
Marston Gate.